Paolo Segneri, Giovanni Battista Roberti, Louis Le Valois

A little treatise on the little virtues

Written originally in Italian

Paolo Segneri, Giovanni Battista Roberti, Louis Le Valois

A little treatise on the little virtues
Written originally in Italian

ISBN/EAN: 9783337228934

Printed in Europe, USA, Canada, Australia, Japan

Cover: Foto ©Andreas Hilbeck / pixelio.de

More available books at **www.hansebooks.com**

A LITTLE TREATISE

ON

THE LITTLE VIRTUES

WRITTEN ORIGINALLY IN ITALIAN,

BY FATHER ROBERTI,

OF THE SOCIETY OF JESUS.

TO WHICH ARE ADDED

A LETTER ON FERVOR,

BY FATHER VALLOIS, S. J.

AND

MAXIMS

FROM AN UNPUBLISHED MANUSCRIPT OF

FATHER SEGNERI, S. J.

ALSO,

DEVOTIONS TO THE SACRED HEART OF JESUS.

———◆———

NEW YORK:

THE CATHOLIC PUBLICATION SOCIETY

126 NASSAU STREET.

TO

Madame Catherine Roberti,

RELIGIOUS IN THE CONVENT

OF ST. BENEDICT,

IN PADUA,

BY HER UNCLE,

FATHER ROBERTI, S. J.

TO THE READER.

Tꜰᴇ Author of the little work now offered to the public, is very well known in Italy by his ascetic writings, and deserves to be universally so, as those who read his "Little Treatise on the Little Virtues" will readily admit. The ABBE ROBERTI, gifted with great refinement of mind and delicacy of feeling, has succeeded in giving to a subject which, at the first glance, may appear dry, a singular interest and unspeakable charm, by the graces of his style and beauty of his language.

To benefit, in a spiritual way, the numerous religious communities spread, happily, through our own and other countries, is the only motive which has engaged us to publish this little work; for it seemed that we could put nothing more useful or consoling into the hands of persons who live together in one house, and are united under one rule.

Yet its usefulness is not confined to communities alone; for, though it is written for a young religious, it suits equally well all ages and all conditions of society.

5

CONTENTS.

CONTENTS.

SHORT MEMOIR

OF THE

ABBE ROBERTI.

JOHN BAPTIST ROBERTI was born on the 4th of March, 1719, at Bassano, of a patrician family. His parents sent him, when very young, to Padua, to be formed to virtue and learning in the school of the Jesuits, whose success in the education of youth is so universally acknowledged. His studies being ended, he demanded and obtained admission into the Society. After his noviciate, he was destined to the employment of teaching, and held, successively, a professor's chair with distinction at Placenza, Brescia, Parma, and Bologna; but it was in this last town that he acquired the greatest celebrity. During eighteen years that he filled the chair of philosophy, his

9

lectures were attended every day by a numerous auditory, who pressed round him
with eagerness to receive the lessons of
wisdom which fell from his lips.   His lectures were interrupted in 1773 by the sup-
pression of his Order, to which he was
strongly attached.   The necessity of sepa-
rating from his religious brethren afflicted
him profoundly.   He returned into the
bosom of his family, where he continued to
devote himself to study, and the practice
of the duties of his state.   Enjoying the
affections of his relatives, and the esteem
of his fellow-citizens, he died at the age
of sixty-eight, carrying with him the
blessings and regrets of the poor and afflicted, to whom he had been a father.   The
last words which he addressed to his nephew
were these : " Remember that every thing
is vanity in this world."

FATHER ROBERTI has left a great number
of moral and religious works.

A LITTLE TREATISE

ON

THE LITTLE VIRTUES.

I.

WHEN, in the course of the last year, you made to God the entire and public consecration of yourself, I published, on the solemnity of which you were the object, the eulogium of St. Jane Frances de Chantal, with "a Letter on Happiness." Now that you are about to consummate your sacrifice by the holy vows, I will not remain an idle spectator, satisfied with interiorly participating in your joy, but giving no outward expression to my feelings: I will not ascend to the temple with empty hands.

I offer you on this day, another

little ascetic work, containing a panegyric of St. Francis de Sales, with some observations on the Little Virtues.*

This gift is not unconnected with the former; and let us hope, that in heaven, St. Jane Frances will appreciate it, and that she will rejoice to see you, her devoted servant, become better acquainted with her Master and Father. As in the panegyric of St. Francis de Sales, and still more in the works of the holy bishop, you will often find the "Little Virtues" mentioned, and their practice most warmly recommended, I think it may be of use to give you, in a few words, a definition of them, and trace the true and simple character of those virtues, the continual practice of which is so suitable and

---

* The translator, encouraged by the success of this treatise, will in a short time publish the Letter and Panegyric here alluded to.

so necessary in the religious state which you are about to embrace.

II.

And first, what are these Little Virtues? They are numberless; but I will give you an abridged enumeration of them,—certain indulgences, forgiving the faults of others, though we are not sure of the same pardon for ourselves; a certain dissimulation, which seems not to observe the most glaring defects—quite opposed, as you may perceive, to the unenviable merit of discovering those that were hidden; a certain sympathy, which appropriates the pains of the unhappy to lessen them; and a certain gaiety, which adopts the joys of the happy to increase them; a certain suppleness of mind, which embraces without hesitation all that is judicious in the ideas of a companion, though the same did not occur to us, and which in consequence applauds his discoveries without envy; a certain solicitude, which forsees the wants of others, to spare them the pain of feeling them, and the humiliation of asking for assistance; a certain liberality of heart, ever ready to do all that it possibly can to oblige, and even when it does but little, would willingly do a great deal; a certain tranquil affability, which listens to the importunate without apparent *ennui*, and instructs the ignorant and stupid without any painful reproaches; a certain urbanity, which in discharging the duties of politeness exhibits, not the graceful dissimulation of the world, but a truly Christian cordiality. All these things, and many others of the same kind, belong to the exercise of the virtues I wish to define. In a word, affability, condescension, simplicity, gentleness, sweetness of looks and actions, sweetness in words and manners,—such are the precious virtues on which my heart impels me to write a little Treatise for your instruction, as well as for my own advantage.

III.

I observe, then, in the first place, that the "Little Virtues" are social virtues, that is to say, extremely useful to all those who live in the society of reasonable creatures. They would be superfluous in the recluse, whose only companions are the savage beast and the wild bird of the woods. Preach to him of fasting, mortification of the flesh, recollection, contemplation, it is all he requires; but for other solitaries it is not so. Wherever there are cloisters and

cells, whose silence must be interrupted by some words, let them be
as brief and as rare as you please;
wherever there is a kitchen to prepare
food, an oven to make bread, a common work-room—in short, wherever
there is an interchange of necessary
services, and consequent words and
signs, all these virtues find their
place. It is certain that without
them, this little world we live in
cannot be well governed, and that
the members who compose it must be
in disorder and inevitable desolation.
Without them, domestic peace is lost
—that first of comforts, amidst the
sorrows and calamities sown so thick
in this dark valley of our pilgrimage.
Oh! how miserable is the dwelling in
which their exercise is neglected!—
parents and children, brothers and
sisters, masters and servants, all in
discord. Without love for the Little
Virtues, how will it be possible for

two or three women to live under the
same roof, but in perpetual warfare?
If it were not profane to cite a
comedy, (and who will deny that a
comedy may be rational, or that truth
may be taught with a smiling face,)
I would tell you that a distinguished
author, who yet lives, introduces on
the scene a mother and her daughter-
in-law; the former, of an ancient
family, who brought to her husband
nobility without wealth; the latter,
whose family was of more recent
date, brought to her husband great
wealth, but not nobility. As they
are both quarrelsome and ill-tem-
pered, they fail in cementing even
the slightest link of friendship, and
the conclusion of the piece is their
separation; one being to live on the
upper story, and the other on the
lower floor of the house, with this
precaution, carefully to avoid all
salutations, or even meetings, as

things too dangerous to their domestic peace.

When going through the streets
of the town, I pass by certain mansions, where I know the minds of all
the inmates to be in tumult from internal dissensions, I feel a longing
desire to affix an inscription on their
porticos: already I write it, and engrave it on my soul: an inscription
never to be effaced, and to be read by
all whenever they enter or go out of
the house. It is taken from St. Paul,
and is comprised in two words:
supportantes invicem—bear with each
other.*

To pass from comedy to the sorrowful tragedies of real life, negligence
in fulfilling the delicate duties connected with the Little Virtues has
been the source, in more than one
instance, of serious scandals and ob-

* Eph. vi. 2.

stinate hatred. Any one conversant with the history of the world, knows that most important events have originated from the most trivial causes: from a spark a great fire has blazed forth. The mutual hatred entertained between two ministers of state, and which became celebrated by its consequences, originated in the omission of a title, and a signature placed too high in a letter. A pair of gloves given at an auspicious moment, and a cup of tea overturned on a footstool, had much to do with the great war which opened this century;* and the refusal of a visit which one lady owed to another was one of the principal causes of the last war, which we used to hear of in our infancy.

But without reading history, or entering into politics, which concern

---

* The eighteenth.

me very little at this moment, and
you still less, we can observe the
private manners of our own times.
We will find that an indiscreet gos-
siping, an imprudent silence, forget-
ing some act of politeness, has, among
persons most closely connected, given
rise to interminable law-suits, fatal
divisions of patrimony, and ruinous
separations of families.   Too often
have I been present at violent and
long disputes, where each party as-
sailed the other without mercy, because a piece of news announced by
one was denied by the other.   How
many persons think themselves deeply wounded in their honor, if every
word they choose to say or write is
not believed with implicit faith.   In
their opinion, to be the first to know
all the frivolous news of the town or
province, is a mark of superior clever-
ness and intelligence; and they agi-
tate and harass themselves to obtain

this silly distinction, when it would be so easy to preserve a perfect calm by some act of our Little Virtues. In directing my attention to what regards you more immediately, I do not fear to affirm, that these virtues, useful to all, are for you absolutely necessary. It is not rare in the world to hear persons declaim with bitterness against the religious state, and deplore the fate of those who embrace it, because if they happen to meet a companion with a disagreeable temper, and a character quite opposed to their own, separation is impossible, and they must endure this annoyance all their lives. I am not in the habit of lending a willing ear to the conversation of libertines; but in the present instance, as I have a great love for truth, I must acknowledge that the objection is not groundless. Yes, it is so. In the world a secular never wants a remedy

against domestic vexations : he leaves
his home—he occupies himself with
various objects—he distracts and di-
verts himself in a thousand different
ways. The religious man, also, is
not without a resource : he has always at hand the most universal and
most efficacious of any—that of meeting new faces in a change of mon-
asteries. But the nun, by her state destined to perpetual enclosure, finds her
associates as permanent as her resi-
dence; she will then be often employed with a sister of uncongenial
mind, in the sacristy, refectory,
infirmary, or other offices. Now in
this continual succession of ordinary
occupations, the constant exercise of
the social virtues becomes absolutely
necessary.

Religious women, on whom the
door is happily closed to an infinity
of other dangers, cannot shut out
this one of which I speak; but let

not this consideration make them
conceive the less esteem of their holy
state. Were I speaking to a community assembled to hear me, I
would propose to them a doctrine
grounded on solid principles of moral
and ascetic theology. I would dis-
tinguish the temptations from which
we must fly, from those which we
must encounter. To temptations
caused by objects that are pleasing,
we must always turn our back with
fear; but not so with temptations
arising from disagreeable objects;
these we often may and even ought
to face courageously. On this point
many allow themselves to be deceived
by passion, even in prayer. Let us
give an example. A person feels too
tender a friendship growing within
her—already her conscience warns
her to renounce it. She goes to
prayer, and beseeches God to grant
her, not the strength to get rid of

this affection, but strength not to offend him in preserving it. This is an illusion and an abuse of prayer: because here it is not the grace of resisting, but the grace of flying, she ought to have asked. It would be quite otherwise if this person had a decided coldness for a companion; because the rules of prudence always held in view, she may seek the object of her aversion and try to gain her friendship. From these principles I would draw the conclusion, that religious persons have no reason to complain of enclosing within their walls a crowd of similar little temptations to *ennui* and impatience, but that they ought to attack and vanquish them by the acts which are their contraries.

I am so convinced of this truth, that if after the exhortation, the fear of failing sometimes in this so necessary sweetness and gentleness, urged

one of the nuns to wish to converse
no more with the others, and that
she consulted me on the subject, I
would say, "take care, my dear
sister, of acting thus; on the contrary, make an effort over yourself—
go and treat kindly and obligingly
with every one. If you happen to
fall into some fault against charity,
from the evil of impatience draw the
treasure of humility; humble yourself at the feet of Almighty God—
ask him with earnestness to help you;
rise and take again part in the conversation, with a will to behave
better." My counsel would certainly agree with that given by St. Jerome to a young person of a very
distinguished family, who, from a
desire of perfection, wished to separate from her mother: the latter was
of a difficult temper, and her pur-
suits were very different from those
of her daughter. "My mother,"

(she writes to her director,) "is an ob-
stacle to my good resolutions, and
opposes my pursuing the pious course
of life which we arranged I should
follow." And St. Jerome replies:
"It matters little, O my daughter,
were your mother even such a person
as you describe her; continue to live
with her, for you will thus reap
greater merit and a richer recompense.

IV.

The Little Virtues, by their nature, are sheltered from all danger.
Their security lies even in their lit-
tleness. They are not pompous, because they are exercised on trivial
objects; they are practised almost
without giving you the reputation of
being virtuous, and our neighbor
exacts rather than admires them.

The pardon of a serious injury may, even humanly speaking, be something glorious, but to forgive a slight offence, excites no admiration. To the insolent wretch who strikes you on one cheek, calmly to present the other, is an evangelical action, which astonishes; but to make no remark on the awkward hand which spoils your work or injures your garments, passes unnoticed. The Little Virtues are then not exposed to vain glory, which only attacks a certain class of spiritual riches. Besides vain glory has nothing to rob where nothing is exhibited, where every thing, if I may so express it, is kept locked up and well secured. The Little Virtues are practised in secret, in obscurity; vain glory is, as it were, ignorant of them, and cannot lay snares to destroy their merit. The missionary, whose holy word moves a whole population, and

whose praises are echoed by the sighs
and groans of an entire people, may
fear the enthusiastic admiration of
the multitude, and, in the fervor of
his zeal, dread the frauds and thefts,
nay, even the rapine and open violence of vanity. But here everything passes in silence between the
conscience and God. Those who are
present do not often perceive why we
have said one word, and they cannot
know why we have suppressed another; they do not penetrate the
mind to read there that the matter is
seen in a different light—they cannot
penetrate to the heart to know that
it is felt in a different manner. Besides our Little Virtues are practised
often with such rapidity, that vain
glory has neither time nor means of
seizing them in their flight. A glance
of the eye, a gesture, a word—and
the act of virtue is effected.

Works of piety are usually under-

taken with upright intentions, but
then this pure and right intention
weakens by degrees, and is lost insensibly. I think there never was a
preacher of the Gospel with so little
virtue as to begin a sermon from the
sole motive of vain glory, and who
would not recite at least the *exordium*
with a pure intention : the danger is
found in the conclusion, and at the
end of his discourse, if his auditory
applaud him with warmth and viva-
city. St. Gregory the Great was a
most learned Pope, and a man of rare
merit. He had completed a ponder-
ous volume of his works, when one
day sitting at his table in his library.
and examining the mass of those
splendid pages piled carefully one
upon another—laborious fruits of so
many meditations on the holy Scrip-
tures—of so many lectures of the
Fathers of the five preceding centuries—he felt his heart swelling little

by little with a vain complacency.
Laying down his pen, he dwells de-
liciously on thoughts of honor and
applause, imagining (as I fancy) that
his book is favorably received at
court; that in the Greek Churches it
adds a new lustre to the name of the
Roman Pontiff; that crossing the
seas it is regarded in converted Eng-
land as an honorable monument of
him whose zeal has effected this
happy change, and whom it already
looks upon as a father; together
with other imaginings of the kind.
At length, struck with a vivid ray of
celestial light, our saint returns to
himself, and collecting before the
Lord his humbled mind, he cries out
with a profound sigh, and his eyes
raised to heaven: "What is all
this? what do I feel within me?
My God! you know with what a pure
intention I set myself to compose
my book of Morals, and now by

what delusion of vanity, insensibly stolen over me, do I find all the ideas of my mind and affections of my heart perverted? At the moment when, after so much watching and labor, I was ready to stretch out my hand and pluck the ripe fruit of merit, it disappears before me, and I lose all. Oh! no, my Lord and God! source of all good, to thee alone belong light and power, to thee alone then be honor and glory for endless ages of ages."

The saints themselves are then exposed to temptations of vain glory in their difficult enterprises, and which require a long time to perfect. It is not so with the Little Virtues; they are sheltered from those dangers by their very nature.

Their security flows also from another source; We certainly will not find in them that inordinate self-love and self-will which would fain domineer everywhere; vices which spoil the merit of fasting and the hair-cloth, as masters of spiritual life are fully aware of. The Little Virtues are exercised almost against our nature; for beware of thinking that their practice consists only in rendering services or manifesting affectionate feelings to an amiable and beloved person; no, this is rather following our natural inclination, and the impulse of friendship. Their true exercise consists in enduring the disagreeable and ungrateful, though in the bottom of our hearts we feel all our little passions in a ferment. It is so true that they do not second the views of self-love, that their choicest flowers are gathered precisely at the moment when we disguise an antipathy, a weariness, conceal an aversion, or an interior opposition of sentiment. In their exercise it is permitted to dissemble; and hypocrisy of a new kind becomes praiseworthy. By dissembling I mean, overlooking a want of attention, a want of respect, some mark of contempt, as if one had neither eyes nor ears. By a praiseworthy hypocrisy I mean, a calm on the countenance, when the heart is in a storm; I mean cool language, when the feelings are hot; I mean absolute silence, when we are strongly moved to give clamorous vent to our irritation. But we must take particular care that, with all this constraint, we preserve such a natural and easy manner, that nothing of what is passing within appears without. In fine, patience requires for its perfection, that we never suffer a cloud of sorrow to rise, or at least to condense upon our brow.

V.

The Little Virtues are ordinary virtues, that is to say, of frequent and daily use, common to all times and conditions of life. Certain virtues, or at least some of their acts, are rare. Many persons pass a long life without sustaining any serious injury in their character, or without being exposed to any atrocious calumny. Assuredly they who would wait for such rude trials to exercise their patience, may wait very long. Nevertheless, this is the illusion of many pious persons. During their prayers they conjure up the strongest suppositions, and fancy themselves in circumstances requiring the greatest heroism of courage; they dream of extraordinary cases of extraordinary virtue; they amuse their imagination, and suffer it to wander through

these magnificent adventures. By
dint of painting virtue, they look
upon themselves as virtuous; and,
passing from fancy to reality, think
they have arrived at perfection. Thus
do they go from their imaginary prayer, full of imaginary patience, but, in
fact, as irascible and unmanageable
as when they entered their oratories.

Occasions of practising our ordinary virtues are met without being
sought for, and during our whole
life. I once heard it quoted from an
ancient ascetic author, that chastity
was the virtue of the young, and
obedience the virtue of the old. And,
in truth, for a novice who joins a religious institution,—at her first en-
trance, during those open-hearted
years of spiritual infancy, when all
its customs are so new to her, every
thing persuades her to be respectful
and obliging to the elder members,
and obedient to superiors. But the

whole weight of obedience is felt
when an elderly Religious of great
authority must submit her views
to a superior, perhaps less distinguished than herself for soundness of
judgment.

None of these distinctions occur in
the practice of the Little Virtues;
they suit equally well every condition
of society, and every epoch of our
lives, every day in the year, and
every hour in the day. It would be
hard to find a case in which we may
exclude the practice of some one or
other of them, at least for any con-
siderable time. Thus, to give a
single example: want of money may
prevent us giving an alms, but we
can always refuse it in a virtuous
manner, that is to say, refuse it with
sweetness blended with compassion.
Another reflection occurs to me:
the Little Virtues can be exercised
when the practice of many others are

interdicted. If one among you be indisposed, she cannot go to choir, she cannot share the labors of the others, she cannot fast, sometimes she cannot say the office even in private; but she can always display a serene resignation, submitting calmly to the directions of physicians and surgeons, asking with humble voice and manner the services of her sisters, and receiving them with a grateful smile. And this consideration has increased force, if we pass from the infirmity of the body to the infirmity of the soul. The soul, from time to time, languishes and falls sick. Then come days of gloom, or at least some quarter hours' of darkness; every object seems shrouded in sadness, and the whole world one scene of *ennui;* under different forms we find this weariness nestled in the very centre of our hearts, so that we become insupportable to ourselves.

Languor weighs down the body, sloth enervates the mind, fervor is extinct, the imagination troubled, the heart cold, relish of devotion lost; prayer, pious reading, spiritual conference, bring no relief; it seems that nothing more remains for us in this world than the weight of sufferings without the comfort of hope. Now in this painful situation of mind and heart, when the exhausted soul is scarce able to fulfill its duties, is the auspicious moment for the exercise of virtue, and the chosen moment for the meritorious exercise of those we advocate. O! God of heaven, who soundest the heart and seest the thoughts, of what weight in that balance wherein thou weighest our merits, would be, at such a moment, an answer given with sweetness to some useless question—an assistance rendered graciously to some frivolous undertaking! These virtues, then,

are the virtues of all times and
seasons.

VI.

The Little Virtues are rational virtues. I must explain this term. Assuredly all the virtues are founded in
reason, and though some among them
are superior to reason, they always
enlighten and perfect it. I only
mean to say that the practice of those
we treat of is truly philosophical,
even humanly speaking; that is to
say, they are so suitable to our
nature and circumstances, that reason assisted solely by its own light,
cannot fail to appreciate them highly,
As to bear with our neighbor is the
object proposed in the exercise of
these cherished virtues, I will suggest
some motives drawn from reason alone,
which may help us to endure the
failings of those who surround us.

The first motive exists in the weakness of the person we suffer from. Yes, the weakness of our neighbor is a recommendation in her favor. We have, for example, to endure a person who is suspicious, who sifts and examines every word, and interprets against herself everything she hears and sees; for her, every fly that buzzes through the air is an elephant which will fall and crush her; every spark a fire in which she is to be consumed. Truly this race of suspicious gentry is very fatiguing: always harsh and disagreeable, always surrounded by their own gloomy imaginings, they oblige you, when you treat with them, to take a thousand minute precautions, and watch over every look, action, and gesture; and after all your pains you have the mortification of seeing that your efforts have been unavailing. Yet these must be borne with, precisely on account of their weakness ; because as their suspicions are unjust, they are sufficiently punished by their very suspicions themselves. Ah ! if we knew what poison to the heart is all this distrust, at once so varied and so constant ! did we know what sorrowful nights and days of bitterness it causes to the unhappy being who is its victim ! could we know how she tries to dissipate the clouds that envelope her, and prove herself in the wrong. But such is her nature, (if I may so speak,) that she soon falls back into her doubts, and embraces again what she at first rejected. It is then consistent with common sense that we endure such characters, because their weakness and the imperfection of their character render them worthy of compassion.

To give another example. A sister is naturally hasty and quarrelsome— let us bear her infirmity, which dis-

pleases her more than it injures us.
A very little puts her in a passion;
granted, but she is as easily appeased;
her good heart makes her readier to
make peace than to give battle;
having returned to her cell, she is
more vexed with herself than with
her companion; at her examen of
conscience she asks pardon of God
for her fault, and takes the earliest
opportunity to beg the same of her
sister. Let us have patience with
her then, and not increase her confusion by our resentful sensibility.

May I take a third example from
material objects. One of your companions has bad health, or at least
thinks she has. This disposition
seldom excites compassion and is still
less pitied, if being really delicate,
she makes herself more so, by an excessive desire to be cured; whereas,
it often happens, nothing helps so
much to restore lost strength, as to

make rational use of that portion
which is left to us. Now here is a
person to be borne with ; and if the
care of her health be too scrupulous,
let us, I repeat it, still bear with her,
because this excess is a new weakness
and a real malady. These consider- -
ations ought to be dwelt on particularly by persons in communities. of
robust health and strong constitu-
tions, who having no experience of
internal suffering, find it hard to
believe in the wants of others, and
little disposed to shew them any indulgence, above all if the malady be
hidden, and give no external indica·
tion of its existence. As to those
hidden ailments, to be persuaded
that the minute attentions which the
sister allows herself, and which offend
the eyes of the community, are not
the result of a blameable delicacy,
we would do well to make a calcula-
tion, and balance the comforts she

procures with those she denies herself, on account of her health; we
should find that the loss is often
greater than the gain: and would
self-love, so clear-sighted on its own
interests, easily fall into such a mis-
take? More than once it has happened, that persons who appeared
too nice, and as it were disgusted
with the ordinary food of the community, so as to incur universal cen-
sure, have in the end, and when it
was too late, given evident demon-
stration that they were attacked with
some serious internal and incurable
malady.

The second motive of endurance
is, if I may so speak, the lightness
of the faults we have to bear. You
live among a class of distinguished
females, exempt by their birth and
education from many faults; besides
they are good religious, who shed
the sweet odor of Jesus Christ around

them. The love of perfection, and its daily study, render very trivial in them, the imperfections which escape from human frailty. Where shall we find a society of men or women who are without a shadow of defect, not in the eyes of our Lord, but even in our own eyes? It would not be hard even in a very regular community, to find a person (and I take this example at random) who would unceasingly descant on the nobility of her origin and the grandeur of her family, who continually congratulates herself and requires your felicitations, because she thinks every thing that belongs to her is good, excellent, perfect; thus, her works are the best executed, her clothes are the neatest, her cell is the best kept, her watch is the most exact—infallible in its indications. On the contrary, it is not harder to find some one else, equally annoying

by her continual lamentations over
herself and nearly the whole human
race ; who has nothing to tell you of
the past but sorrowful adventures, of
the present but the pains she endures,
and of the future but those she is
dreading; who sighs continually over
the disorders of the age, and whose
zeal is far from being purified from
all bitterness. How is it possible to
regulate our conduct with regard to
characters so different? It is related
that formerly their existed two sages,
one of whom wept continually, and
the other laughed without ceasing.
They have still their imitators. Let
us endeavor to be one and the other
by turns; we will weep after having
laughed, and laugh after weeping;
that is to say, we will weep with
those that weep, we will laugh with
those that laugh ; and this not to
flatter, but to edify; for after all,
this is the maxim of St. Paul: "Re-

joice with those that rejoice, and mingle your tears with those who weep."*

The third motive is, not only the lightness of the fault, but the absence of all fault. We must support many things in our neighbor quite independent of habit, of reflection, unconnected with any kind of virtue, things indifferent in themselves and to which no blame can be attached. Such are the outlines of the features, a certain expression of countenance, a tone of voice, a manner of holding the body not according to our taste; we may also place in this list the diversity of characters and their opposition to ours. One is naturally serious and the other gay; one is timid and the other daring; one is pusillanimous, the other magnanimous. Reason demands that we live in peace in the

* Gaudere cum gaudentibus, flere cum flentibus. Rom. xii. 15.

midst of these natural discords, and that we accommodate ourselves to the humors of others by the pliancy of our patience. To complain of this diversity of characters would be as foolish as to fret because another liked a fruit or a sweetmeat that was not according to our taste.

The fourth motive of forbearance is, that we ourselves require to be borne with. No one in this world is so wise or so accomplished in perfections, that he can at all times dispense with the indulgence of others. To-day, I must bear patiently with some person, and to-morrow I may be an exercise of patience to that person, or some other. What injustice would it be, to exact respect and consideration from others, and to return only haughtiness and rudeness?

Do not say: "As for me, I understand and observe all the courtesies of life, and it would be hard to find

more refined good-nature than my
actions exhibit." It will ever remain true, that we easily flatter ourselves on the point of good manners,
but it is very difficult to unite the
various qualities which constitute
genuine politeness, in all its perfection. Nobody sees the blots that
disfigure his own face; to others
alone it belongs to judge whether we
are as amiable as we think ourselves.
All that we can know is, that we
study to become so; and even this
study may savor of affectation, and
displease! In writing thus to you,
my dear sister, I am aware that a
character so gentle as yours, will
scarcely once in a month give subject
of complaint, while others will every
day of their lives furnish matter for
charitable forbearance. But take
notice, when I wish to show how just
it is to support our neighbor's defects
because our own must be supported,

I do not mean to propose a contract
of strict equality, but only some
kind of compensation;—no, in this
case it is not justice, jealous of its
rights, but generous charity we look
for. For reflect, that this is the fruit,
and, I would almost say, the lawful
usury of this mode of proceeding,
since it is the true secret of making
ourselves beloved. Let us then stop
both our ears to the detestable principles of those who would recommend
pride and resentment; because, say
they, the haughty are respected, and
care is taken not to affront those who
never forgive an injury. Respect
gained on such terms resembles much
that of which the nettle was so proud.
I met the fable in an ancient work.
She insulted not only the lowly
plants and pretty flowers of the
meadow, because, by their excessive
humility, they let themselves be
trodden under foot by all, but even

attacked the poppy, which, growing
high, yet bent its head too conde-
scendingly to the sun and wind,
while she stood erect and covered
with leaves, in spite of cold and heat,
and made herself so respected, that
no one dared to touch her. I suppose
not one among you would be ambi-
tious of the glory of the nettle. I
do not envy even that of the rose,
when she is indiscreet enough to
wound with her thorns.

The fifth motive for bearing with
our neighbor is, the link that unites
us with the person we must endure.
If I were treating this point with
secular persons, observe, I would say
to them, that your patience is exercised in your own family, and towards those of your own blood. I
would then exhort a son to bear with
a quarrelsome mother—a husband to
endure an arrogant wife—the sister
to support the caprices of a brother.

Remember, I would add, that domestic broils are much more painful than trials that come from without. David, who had a heart so tender and sensitive, complains in the bitterest terms of what he suffered from his own family: *"Lord,"* he cries out, prostrate on the earth, *"these are my brethren, and nevertheless they regard me as a stranger; we came from the womb of the same mother, and they consider me an alien from a distant country."**

I need say nothing of all this to you, who have quitted your house and family; who have, with a noble emulation, abandoned your father, your mother, and your brethren. But still, if you have broken the old ties of flesh and blood, you have formed new ones more spiritual, and born of charity. The consecrated

* Extraneus factus sum fratribus meis, et peregrinus filiis matris meæ.—Ps. lxviii.

virgins among whom you have fixed your abode, are your spiritual sisters —daughters of the same father, St. Benedict—inheritors of the same maxims, bound together by the same rules; they ought then to be very dear to you in Jesus Christ. Your cloister is become your country, and even your family. Your holy companions form with you a strict and new kind of citizenship and relationship; they have thence a particular right to be loved by you, and to gather in abundance the delicious fruits of those precious virtues on which I have delighted to expatiate in this letter—I may call it rather a treatise, as it has now reached to such a length as almost to deserve that title. If it happens, then, that any of your companions do not please you much, and offend you a little, say at the very moment she annoys you, she is my sister, I pardon her, and yet more,

I desire to embrace her with the kiss of peace.

How noble was the language of Abraham to Lot! They were two powerful lords, rich in flocks of sheep and oxen, of asses and of camels. It often occurred that their herdsmen quarreled on the subject of pasturage and water for the animals. Let us separate, said Abraham to Lot, with a calm and cordial mien; go to which side you please—choose the pastures which appear to you most fertile and agreeable—if you take the left, I will go towards the right; and if you choose the right, I will take the left. *Between us and our dependants there should be no contest, for* (oh! the powerful and touching reason,) *we are brothers.** And since we recall this benevolence, which St. Paul calls fraternal charity, (charitas fraterni-

* Fratres enim sumus.—Gen. xiii. 8.

tatis,) and St. Peter the love of our brethren, (amor fraternitatis,) I am going to make my last remark to you on the subject of which we treat.

VII.

The Little Virtue are sublime and divine virtues. I am now sorry that I called them little virtues, but the expression was taken from St. Francis de Sales. They are only little, because they relate to little objects—a word, a gesture, a look, a civility; but if we examine the principle in which they originate, and the end to which they tend, they are great and noble. They are little virtues indeed, but they make a man greatly virtuous. In matter of virtues, it is not how much is done that we consider. The mite of the widow in the Gospel is widely celebrated, and was more

esteemed than the high sounding
alms of the Sanhedrim. St. Peter
did not hesitate frankly to interro-
gate the Saviour of the World on
the reward that would be given to
the Apostles for having abandoned
all things for his love. And what
did these poor fishermen quit! They
left their nets, which perhaps were
not new. It is certain that James
and Andrew were seen mending the
meshes of their's on the shore, and
that even Peter's broke when he took
some large fishes; but Peter's great
and generous heart would have left a
throne as he left his bark. A soul
enlightened and careful of her spiritual interests, vivifies and exalts, by
her noble and sublime views, the
smallest acts of virtue; she desires
to perform heroic ones. The exercise
of our beloved virtues is for the true
Christian, a continual exercise of
charity towards his neighbor; and

charity to our neighbor is the charity
of God, honored in our neighbor;
for God, in assuring us that he has
made man to his own image, desires
that we should have Himself always
present to our mind. The sentiment,
then, which should animate these
virtues for us, who are disciples of
the Gospel, is supernatural charity,
of which they are, as it were, the
coloring and the lustre; and this is
what renders them sublime and divine virtues, and eminently meritorious.

They are divine also, as being in-
sinuated by the divine precepts and
divine examples of our master, Jesus
Christ. God always approved of
meekness. Even in the old law—a
law of severity and fear—he enters
into minute details full of gentleness
and benignity. And who is ignorant
that sweetness is the proper character
of the evangelical law, the law of

grace and love? In Jesus Christ nothing could be little—all is worthy of our humble and profound adorations. I invite you, then, to meditate on his private life, and certain small, almost imperceptible traits of charity for our neighbor, that are not always taken notice of in ordinary meditations.

Jesus Christ came into the world to redeem and instruct us. Of three and thirty years which he lived, he passed thirty in an obscure country town, under a poor and humble roof, submissive, obedient, retired, laborious. All this for your instruction as for ours, because the domestic and laborious life is that which is most common to the human race. He was willing that his precursor, John the Baptist, *should eat no bread nor drink wine,* because he was to preach penance in the desert; but for himself, inhabiting towns, he made use of bread and wine, though the Pharisees reproached him with it. One c this designing sect invited him dinner, probably with a malicious intention, as we may conclude by what happened during the repast. Still Jesus accepts the invitation. It was to this feast that Magdalen penetrated; and, while she washes his feet with her tears, and wipes them with her hair, he sees disapproving murmurs brooding in the inmost soul of the Pharisee. Take notice, he does not say a word to excuse himself, but undertakes the defence of the penitent, whose heart was at that moment overflowing with the most lively compunction. Another woman, guilty of a great crime, is presented before him, and he absolves her. The harsh masters of the synagogue who are present, are scandalized; he bends down towards the earth, and then writes silently with

his finger in the dust the sins of each
one; they disappear, one by one,
under various pretexts. I do not
now consider his mercy to the sinner,
but his gentleness towards those rigid
doctors, whom he could have reproached with so many crimes loudly
and to their face; he is content to
warn, without confounding them.
An inhabitant of a city comes to
visit him in the obscurity of the
night; he seems to blush at rendering the homage due to his doctrine.
His timidity does not discourage
Jesus Christ, and as this pusillanimous person has an upright heart, he
welcomes him, converses with him,
instructs him, and receives him as a
disciple. He is called to a dying
servant, and he goes. To prevail on
Jesus to pay a visit to the house of a
military man, some of the most
worthy among the Jews who besought
him, gave him to understand that

this officer loved their nation, and
had constructed a synagogue for their
use. (*Diligit gentem nostram, et syn-
agogam ipse ædificavit nobis.*) And
Jesus Christ yields to these honest
motives, drawn from the love of
country. After curing the dying
servant of the officer at the request
of others, he raises to life and restores
to a desolate widow a beloved son,
without any intercession being made
to him ; moved alone by the tears of
the mother. He accosts her of himself, and in a tone which promises a
miracle ; cease, he says, with divine
sweetness and grace, cease to weep!
and, in a moment, he that was a
corpse springs from the bier into his
mother's arms. A man of the law,
in a haughty and contentious style,
one day asked him : Who is my neighbor? Jesus Christ gives him a satis-
factory answer, with meek tranquillity. But, behold! a woman of Sa-

maria presents herself before him, and, wishing to play the theologian, discusses on which mountain public worship ought to be paid to God. Our Lord instructs this schismatic. It was precisely to convert her, that he had left the town under the rays of a burning sun, and awaited her arrival at the well. The Samaritans, obstinately attached to their schism, would not receive him in one of his journeys, because he appeared to be traveling towards Jerusalem. You know that they had separated themselves from this city and its temple, where alone it was lawful to offer sacrifice. Besides, they had driven away the persons whom he sent before to prepare a lodging for him. To refuse hospitality, and even a passage through their country—what obduracy! Even James and John—that soul so meek and amiable—were indignant, and wished for fire from

heaven to punish them; but Jesus
gently reproaches them, that they did
not know the spirit of love that he
came to shed upon the earth. Do
children desire to approach that they
may gaze on him at their ease, and
perhaps kiss his hand? He makes
his disciples give place, who tried at
first to repulse them. He calls these
little ones to him, and embraces them.
Does he enter the house of death,
where all are in tears? He weeps
himself. If he goes to a marriage,
where all is bridal joy, he works a
miracle to increase their happiness;
and note, that this change of water
into exquisite wine was his first
miracle. He thus spares the master
of the house the mortification of having no more wine to produce at a
solemn banquet, where everything
delicate and rare should appear in
abundance. One day the crowd
thronged so close about him to hear

him speak, that he was almost overwhelmed. Near the shore there lay
a bark ; he could at the moment have
entered into it, and spoke from thence
to the people assembled on the coast,
but he would first have the consent
of its owner, who was a fisherman.
He asks with civility, his permission
and his assistance, (*rogavit,*) and
then, in recompense, he tells him
to cast his net into the water; and
though this man had not taken a
single fish the whole preceding night,
he now catches of the best kind, and
in such numbers, that two ships are
filled with them. The prodigal son
returns after his wanderings and
misconduct. His father, (and this
father is the Lord—he tells us so
himself,) among other incredible
marks of tender mercy—to spare the
young man the shame of appearing
soiled and tattered before his family
—takes care to have him richly

dressed, before he joins his relations,
to rejoice with them. Impelled by
hunger, many of his disciples plucked
some ears of corn, and sifted them in
their hands on the Sabbath-day.
Their indulgent Master does not re-
primand them; but, on the contrary
defends them against the malignant
remarks of the Pharisees. Once did
the Saviour of the world appear aus-
tere; it was in the instance of the
Chananean woman, who was not a
daughter of Abraham. He answered
her, that he was not come to throw
holy things to dogs—that is to say,
to idolaters. But this was only a
feint, for he wished to grant her request, and give her an opportunity of
making that tender and humble comparison, which he puts upon her lips.
Yes, my Lord, I am, I know, but a
poor contemptible dog; but do not
the little dogs eat the crumbs which

the master lets fall from his table?
She is heard that moment!

The holy women among the Israel-
ites, who assiduously rendered him
those little services necessary for the
preservation of life, with regard to
food and clothing, followed him in
his journeys, and spoke often to him;
Jesus Christ, after his resurrection,
as it were in acknowledgment, visits
them before his very apostles. In a
word, to comprehend how, in the
conduct of our Divine Master, there
was a continual display of affability,
condescension, sweet patience, and
gracious courtesy, it is enough to remember, that he conversed with men
who, before receiving the Holy Ghost,
were ignorant, gross, contradictory,
and presumptuous. He bore with
them all—he loved them all; and,
because John's purer soul deserved
it, to John he allowed the endear-
ments of friendship. Judas, chosen

for an apostle, though unworthy of the honor, received the same privileges as the others at the mysterious repast on the sorrowful eve of his death, when Jesus, steeping a morsel of bread in the dish, hands it to this perfidious miscreant. Oh! could we then have watched, with respectful glance, the eyes and expression of Jesus! how sweetly would we learn to be kind and winning to the harsh and revolting, and to render services to the ungrateful, because to those who are agreeable, and to our friends, every one acts with cordiality.* O! how truly in the whole life of Jesus Christ was verified what was predicted of him! that his meekness and sweetness would be so great, that he

---

* Et si diligitis eos qui vos diligunt, quæ vobis est gratia? Nonne et peccatores diligentes se diligunt? Et si benefeceritis his qui vobis benefaciunt, quæ vobis est gratia? Siquidem et peccatores hoc faciunt.—Luc. vi, 32, 33.

would not extinguish the latent spark
where it yet glowed, nor crush the
bruised reed.

Learn of me, he says, because I am
meek and humble of heart. Learn,
then, beloved sister, this meekness,
which springs from humility, and
terminates in charity. Perhaps, in
reading the title of this treatise, you,
as well as others, conjectured that in
the course of it I would propose
things just and good, but not of
sovereign importance. Yet, I think,
I have pointed out to you true Christian and religious perfection. I am
satisfied to have merely indicated it ;
and, though it would be easy to col-
lect various other topics, and spread
out my remarks over long pages, I
will not add another word, lest,
while I exhort you to bear with the
tiresome, I add, **by** my prolixity, one
more to the list of those you must
endure.

in spirit, because it is the Lord whom you serve." But, my dear sister, I must, in the first place, remind you that when the Apostle exhorts us to fervor, it is not precisely to a sensible fervor. For he speaks of a fervor which resides in the soul, and sensible fervor does not go so far; it dwells in the sensitive appetite. Besides, sensible fervor consists in receiving consolations from God; and St. Paul speaks of a fervor which consists in action and in rendering services to God. In fine, since the Apostle exhorts us, it follows that the matter depends on us. This is not by any means the case in regard to sensible fervor, which so far from depending on us cannot be obtained by any exertion of ours. It is not then of sensible fervor that he speaks; it is of spiritual fervor, which consists in the will, but in a firm, generous, efficacious, ardent, and active

will. This is the fervor of which I
wish to speak to you: and because
the most simple and the best means
to create a love for virtue, is to make
it known, and to represent it such as
it is, I shall give you the portrait of
a fervent soul. If you find any resemblance to yourself in it, I shall
bless God; but if in some points you
find yourself deficient, (and who is
there who is not deficient? and in
how great a degree are not all so?)
I conjure you to labor, either to form
these traits, or to renew them within
you, that so you may be yourself renewed, and Jesus Christ be formed
within you. Permit me to commence
by a comparison, which, though it
may appear to you very sublime, you
can easily understand. For without
wishing to speak in a language too
refined or mystical, it seems to me
that fervor is amongst the virtues of
man, what infinity is amongst the

attributes of God. The infinity of
God is not a particular but a general
attribute, and it is so in two senses.
1st.—Because it contains all other
attributes, and signifies that God
possesses all possible perfections.
2dly.—Because it belongs to each
particular perfection of God, and signifies, not only that God is infinite,
but also that all the perfections of
God are infinite, viz: that his wisdom
is infinite, his power is infinite, his
mercy is infinite: so that to say God
is infinite, is to say that he possesses
an infinity of perfection, and that all
these perfections are infinite. We
may say the same, in some degree, of
fervor. Fervor in man is not a particular but a general virtue, in this
double sense. 1st.—Because it contains all virtues, and that it makes
us acquire and preserve them all.
2dly.—Because it accompanies each
virtue in particular: for we are not

only fervent when we possess fervor, but all our virtues are fervent. Our love of God is fervent, our charity towards our neighbor is fervent, our mortification and our humility are fervent; so that to say a man is fervent, is to say he has all virtues, and that he has no virtue which is not fervent. But what is it that constitutes this fervor, or rather what actions does it make us perform? How does it make us perform them? And for what end? Heaven grant, my dear sister, that you may know this in the end by experience, if you have not sufficiently known it before. Meanwhile I shall explain it to you in a simple but instructive manner. As to the first question, of what a fervent soul does, I reply that she does all she is obliged to, and even more; all that she can, and in some measure more than (naturally speaking) she can do. Strive to penetrate

the sense of the four degrees which
follow; what I shall say will be short,
but substantial, and will contain
many things.

Fervor, in the first place, makes a
soul apply to all her duties, otherwise it would be a mistaken fervor;
and we cannot sufficiently deplore
the illusion of some religious persons,
who neglect the rule which religion
prescribes them, and the ordinary
observances of the community, to at-
tach themselves to particular exercises which are of their own choice.
That is to say, they will do *more* than
God wills, but they will not do *what*
he wills. A fervent religious studies,
above all things, to avoid all the evil
that is forbidden by her state, and to
do all the good that her state enjoins.
Let the evil which she is forbidden
be great or small; let the good which
is ordained be important or trifling;
this is not what she looks to; this

evil she will say is forbidden by God —that suffices; this good work is enjoined by God—that is enough. She regards the smallest sins as extremely great evils, because they offend God, and this only thought gives her a horror of them; she looks on great sins as impossible in regard of her, and this excludes the very idea of committing them. In order to excite herself to the greatest ardor in the practice of the least good work, she looks on it as important, inasmuch as it contributes to the glory of God; and to engage herself indispensably to the practice of the greatest good, she regards it as absolutely necessary, inasmuch as it tends to the greater glory of God. Fidelity in great things appears to her as glorious, and this encourages her to undertake them. Infidelity in smaller things appears to her so much the more shameful, as they are more easily accomplished; and this renders her incapable of failing in them. Hence, she is exact in little things, generous in those which are great, and faithful in both.

Secondly.—After all, this is but the first degree of fervor. Not content with doing all she is obliged to, a fervent soul does much more than her obligations exact from her. She does not only fly from the evil which is forbidden, but she likewise applies herself, as much as is in her power, to prevent any of her actions from being unprofitable. She not only does all the good that is commanded, she strives also to do all that is counseled. It is not by her obligations, but by her power, that she limits her enterprises. When the thought of doing a good action occurs, she does not stop to examine if she is obliged to do it, but only whether she can do it; she does not examine if she can

do it easily, but if she can possibly
do it ; and from the moment that she
finds it absolutely possible, she hesi-
tates no longer, but begins to act : at
whatever price it may cost her, she
will execute it.

Thirdly.—Here, my dear sister, is
one of the most holy dispositions of a
fervent soul. After doing all that
she is strictly obliged to, and going
far beyond it, and doing all that she
can, she yet believes that she does
not do all that she ought, because
while any thing remains which is
possible, *that* she thinks she should
do. Farther, as she knows that her
services can never either equal the
greatness of the Master whom she
serves, or the graces which she has
received from him, whatever she does,
she never believes she has done
enough. She is convinced that whatever she does is nothing in comparison to what she ought to do ; and

this conviction keeps her always in sentiments of the most profound humility, which however does not trouble or afflict her, but which redoubles her fervor, and animates her to undertake every thing.

Fourthly.—I say every thing, and even in some sort what is impossible. For the fervor of love, observes a holy Father, does not stop at what it is obliged to do, or at what it can do, but it goes farther. As the fervent soul believes it a duty to do all that she can, she thinks that she can do all that she desires, and she desires all that the fervor of love inspires her to do. It is not naturally possible that a man should walk on the water, but St. Peter's fervor did not allow him to examine whether it was possible or not: but urged by love, he walked on the water, without thinking on what he walked, being solely occupied with the thought of Him to whom his love carried him. St. Augustine remarks, that Magdalen enquired where they had deposited the body of her Master, in order that, as she said, she might carry it away, and render her last duties to him. But how could a weak, delicate, young woman bear away a dead body, which many men together would find it troublesome to carry? It is thus, says St. Bernard, that love never measures its own forces, but thinks it can do every thing. However, not to speak of things absolutely miraculous, and which we can only admire, it is certain that, even in the ordinary course of life, fervor often leads us to do things which seem in some sort impossible. This happens in four different ways:—

First.—Self-love represents things to us as impossible, which, however, are easy enough; human reason treats as impracticable whatever is difficult, and which, on account of this very difficulty, is very rarely done. But fervor discovers both the illusion of self-love and the errors of human reason, and shews us a possibility where before we saw only insurmountable obstacles.

Secondly.—As fervor animates us extremely, it also gives us much strength; and thus renders that possible to us, which would not be so if we were destitute of it.

Thirdly.—The fervent soul reckons easily on the assistance of God, in circumstances in which the possibility appears to be doubtful. As she is sensible that there is not any thing which she would refuse to God, she also feels a conviction that he will not refuse her any thing. I can do nothing of myself, she will say; but, I can do all things in him who strengthens me. Animated by this confidence, and supported by this

assistance, she undertakes any thing;
and whether it be that the enterprise
is not really so great as it appeared,
or that she is assisted by a miracle of
the Divine omnipotence, success follows the undertaking. When the
great Apostle of the Indies and Japan, Saint Francis Xavier, wished to
cross the tempestuous seas, and to go
forth to preach the Gospel to savage
and barbarous nations, every one was
solicitous for his preservation, and
represented to him the extreme danger to which he exposed himself, the
invincible oppositions he had to encounter, the little appearance there
was of his succeeding, and gaining
to the faith of Jesus Christ a people
who seemed more like wild beasts
than men. If he had argued on the
business himself, according to human
foresight, he would have lost all hope;
but the arm of God is not shortened,
said he; and at this word all his

courage was awakened—he set out, he arrived, and preached; and, so far from not meeting with success, it very much exceeded his expectations. In fine, when things are manifestly impossible to all the forces of nature, fervor, which cannot prudently go so far as to undertake them, at least leads us to desire them. Why have I not the hearts of all those who do not love thee as much as I desire! Why have I not a thousand beings, that so I might endure for thee a thousand deaths! Why cannot I be in a thousand places, to announce thy holy name at the same time in so many different places, and to make thee known to so many different nations! This, my dear sister, is what a fervent soul does: let us now see how she does it—promptly, perfectly, constantly. This is what gives a new value to her actions. Promptly: love gives wings, and fervor is noth·

ing else but a perfect love. The
wings which it gives are so much the
swifter, as they are wings of fire.
Imagine, says the wise man, that fire
is set to a little forest of very dry
reeds: with what swiftness does it
not extend from one extremity to the
other? It is thus that fervor makes
just souls run with speed to every
thing capable of advancing the glory
of God and their own perfection.
Hence, David does not simply say,
that he walked in the paths of the
commandments of the Lord, but that
he ran in them. A fervent religious
does not require much time to delib-
erate on what she has to do, nor much
reasoning to assure her, that it is the
will of God. As she is not under
the influence of any passion which
can prevent her from discovering it,
she immediately perceives what is the
will of God; and from that moment
she does not hesitate: her heart flies

—her hand follows; and it seems to be the same thing for her to see, to will, and to act. If she hears the bell which calls her to rise, to prayer, to examen, to finish recreation, to assemble at a regular observance—at the first stroke she rises—at the first stroke she begins her prayers, her examen,—at the first sound she ceases to speak, and finishes recreation ; she does not delay a moment in going to the place to which God calls her. If superiors order any thing, she hears them at half a word ; and the instant she comprehends their intentions, her fervor does not permit her to defer obeying. The charity of Jesus Christ urges her on ; and the Holy Ghost is, in regard to her, as he was to the Apostles—a spirit of vehemence, which urges and leads her on, and which makes her advance more in a day than others do in a year.

Perfectly : because she is not content with simply doing her actions, she wishes to do them well, and not alone well, but in the best manner possible. All her actions are holy : they are invariably perfect as to their principle, as to their end, and in all their circumstances. Their principle is grace : she follows all its inspirations. Their end is God : she refers all to him. As to their circumstances, it is the subject of her constant attention not to omit any one of them, and to fulfill all justice, in imitation of Jesus Christ, her divine model.

Constantly : though it seems that such an application cannot be of any duration, nevertheless, a soul in which fervor reigns, continues constant, whether it be that it preserves and every day renews the forces of the soul, or that it sweetens all—that it changes labor into rest, pains into delights—in such a manner, that the soul is never wearied, never tired of anything, and consequently never relaxes. As a sensual man, who loves pleasures which he has enjoyed, but continually seeks for new gratifications; so a fervent soul, who loves to labor and suffer for God, never says, it is enough. On the contrary, ever consumed with that ardent thirst after justice, which, according to the Gospel, is the first beatitude of this life—the more she has done, the more she asks to do; the more she has suffered, the more she desires to suffer. This was the sentiment of St. F. Xavier: Yet more, O Lord! he exclaimed, yet more!

O my dear sister, this is the great secret of living happy, but more particularly in the religious profession! We sometimes see religious discontented in their state. They feel all the weight of the yoke which they bear, and carry it with pain. If any

should try to persuade them to do
themselves a little violence, to become more vigilant and exact, to
apply with greater fidelity to the
practices of religion, they think that
this would render their lives still
more unhappy, and their burden
more insupportable. But how much
are they deceived, and why are they
not better informed in what their
true happiness consists! Instead of
taking so much care of themselves,
if they took less, or were not at all
solicitous for their own case; if instead of permitting themselves so
many relaxations, which they look
on as consolations, they placed their
consolation in not seeking any, or in
seeking it in the most strict and regular observance of their duties, how
would they be consoled? They would
begin to relish their vocation, because
they would have the spirit of it; and
this would make them find much

sweetness in the practice of what before was most tiresome, mortifying,
and repugnant to their nature. It is
strange that there is so much difficulty in convincing persons of this
truth, when they have before their
eyes sensible proofs and existing examples. If they applied to those of
the community who appear to them
the most fervent, and enquired of
them if they find their state irksome
and insipid, if they repent having
embraced it, or would exchange it,
if the ordinary exercises of the house
cause them any disgust, if they are
subject to low spirits, to melancholy
and discouragement—Ah! if they
could discover the sentiments of these
souls, they would learn that it is for
them and such as them that the hun-
dred-fold reward is reserved in this
life, as well as the next; and that
there is never a greater calm enjoyed,
a more unalterable peace, nor a purer

joy and happiness, than when a person wishes not to spare herself in any thing in order to please God. In fact, it is only with the intention of pleasing God that a fervent soul acts. In doing all that is possible, and in the best manner, she has Him alone in view : and the considerations which excite in her so much fervor, may also serve to excite the same in you. At one time the fervent soul considers the greatness of God : this only thought—I serve God—transports her in some manner out of herself. I serve God ! whom the Dominations adore — before whom the Powers tremble—to whom the Intelligences are submissive—whom all the blessed spirits glory in serving. If for so great a Master, I should renounce and sacrifice every thing, and should undertake and endure all, would it be too much ? Would it even be enough ? It would be so in regard to my weakness; but in regard of thee and thy greatness, O my God! it would be nothing. At another time she sets before her the goodness of God; she recalls the remembrance of his mercy and his benefits to her; she exclaims with David, " What shall I render thee, O Lord, for all I have received." These words repeated at intervals, and with reflection, are sufficient to enkindle a new flame within her; she would be ashamed to be avaricious towards a God so liberal and even so prodigal in her regard. All that I possess, O Lord, comes from thy bounty, and is thine: for whom else should I employ it but for thee?

At another time she encourages herself by the view of the recompences which God reserves for those who serve Him. If at some moments she finds her fervor abate, a look towards Heaven is enough to renew it.

She knows that all her thoughts, all
her desires, all her words, all her
steps, all her actions, are marked in
the book of life ; that fervor gives
them a particular merit; and that
in proportion to merit, glory is to increase. She has even in this her
hope, the purest views, and in seeking her own interest, it is rather God
than herself that she seeks. For she
knows that the more she shall be
elevated in Heaven, the more she will
love God ; and as she desires to love
God in eternity with the greatest
possible perfection, by love for God
she wishes to amass in time as much
merit as she can, that so she may see
God more clearly and love Him more
ardently for all eternity.

At another time she is urged on by
a holy emulation, either when she
sees with what exactitude and zeal
the great ones of the world desire to
be and are served ; or when she thinks

of what the saints have done, and admires their constancy, their courage, their mortification, their detachment, their continual watchfulness over themselves, their entire submission to every will of God, and their perfect fidelity in accomplishing it; or when she casts her eyes around her, and sees what is every day done by virtuous persons, whose example animates her, and whom she would wish not only to follow in the way of God's service, but to surpass. For it is herein that she believes a holy envy and ambition are permitted her. She rejoices at all the good which others practice; but she would wish to practise still more. She wishes that all creatures who exist were entirely occupied with serving and glorifying God; but she wishes to glorify and serve Him herself more than all of them together. Her avidity is insatiable; and if from the weakness of nature she is only capable of a limited action, her weakness, at least, does not put any limits to her desires.

At another time, retired as she is from the world, placed in the house of God, if she meditates on the obligations of her state—the engagements of the religious profession, she questions herself, as St. Bernard did, why God called her to Himself, what she came to seek in this holy house, what she came to do, and what she has done? This comparison, or rather contrast, between what she ought to have done and what she has done, confounds her. For humility prevents her ever supposing that she has done enough. But this salutary confusion, very far from throwing her into despondency, awakens all her confidence and all her ardor: "I have said it, O my God; this day I begin, and this change is a miracle of thy right hand."

At another time, when thinking of the disorders which reign in the world, and sensibly touched at seeing God so badly served in it, and at so many outrages which he receives, she desires to have it in her power to compensate for them all; and, if she cannot do it entirely, yet she forms the generous resolution, of employing all her powers in doing as much as possible.

Ah! Lord, why cannot I render thee all that glory which the impious refuse thee, who run with impetuosity in the paths of evil! But it is the duty of thy friends to honor thee, O my God! and the more so, since thou hast conferred so great honor on them. In fine, every thing contributes to inflame her love, and to redouble her fervor; for every thing turns to good for souls who love God: and here, my dear sister, is the portrait I present to you. Will it serve as a reproach to you? or, will it be a subject of consolation? It is for you to judge of this at the foot of your crucifix, and to listen humbly to what God shall say to your heart on this subject. Whatever it has heretofore been, and whatever it is at present, may you in these days of salvation obtain a spirit of fervor more active than ever! May it accompany you through the whole course, and in every action of your life!—in your prayers—in your meditations—in your spiritual lectures—in your examens—in your confessions—in your communions—in your conversations—in all your employments. Our Lord is a consuming fire; permit him, my dear sister, to burn—to consume your heart and all its affections. But what do I say? Rather desire this—petition for it—present yourself to him for this purpose. It is thus that you will glorify the Master to whom you have consecrated yourself; that you will edify the community to which you belong ; and that you will advance to that perfection to which you are called.

P. VALLOIS.

A LETTER

WRITTEN TO A RELIGIOUS PERSON DURING HER AN-
NUAL RETREAT.

BY FATHER VALLOIS, S. J.

You are now in solitude; not merely in that habitual solitude in which you have lived, since you renounced the world and embraced the religious state; but a solitude yet more strict, since you are for some days separated from any intercourse with your sisters. The fruit you should derive from this retreat, and to secure which you should strongly animate yourself, is to serve God hereafter with a renewed fervor, and to practise this admirable lesson which the Apostle gave to the first Christians, but which is peculiarly suitable to religious persons: "Be ye fervent

69

MAXIMS:

FROM AN UNPUBLISHED MANUSCRIPT OF F. SEGNERI, OF THE SOCIETY OF JESUS.

1st. If the idea of some difficult mortification, in which, however, there appears nothing absurd or unsuitable, presents itself to your mind, do not say, I cannot, but persuade yourself that, with the help of God, you can do it, though it seems to you above your strength.

2d. If it sometimes happen that you fail in obtaining over yourself some victory which it was your duty to gain, do not fall into depression, but arise with courage, ask of God his grace with greater earnestness, and again attack your enemy, never desisting until you have put him to flight.

3d. Say often to yourself: I have

come into "religion" to do penance, and not to seek my ease: I ought then to be the servant of all, and not their mistress; to study virtue, and not to amuse myself with trifles; to learn humility, and not to comport myself haughtily.'

4th. Engrave deeply in your mind, that if you wish to acquire humility, you must seek humiliations. This is tending to what is solid in virtue. Here no excuse can exist, either from want of health, or permission to perform austerities.

5th. Give the best to others, and seek the worst for yourself. Bear inconveniences yourself willingly to accommodate others. These others are saints, and you are a sinner, but a sinner who wishes to become a saint.

6th. Watch over yourself, and be not disquieted about what others do. You will easily attain to this, if you

accustom yourself to walk with your
eyes cast down, and to keep silence
at the proper times.

7th. Recollect this admirable lesson of St. Teresa: "That to practise
virtue, we must not wait to choose
opportunities, but seize the occasions
that offer."

8th. If you have been offended,
suppress all exterior emotion at the
affront, and interiorly offer some good
work for the person who has offended
you.

9th. Try to do every thing with a
spirit of joy and generosity.

10th. Punctuality to the least sig-
nal!—it is the Lord who calls you.
Do not dispense yourself without
serious necessity.

11th. Every Saturday, beg of
some person in whom you have confidence, to admonish you of your
failings: on the vigils of feasts, ask
pardon of your superior, and beseech

her to tell you of your faults, and
offer yourself for any laborious service she pleases.

12th. If you happen to fail in
charity, fall instantly on your knees
and ask pardon.

13th. Frequently offer the blood
of Jesus Christ for sinners, and for
the many souls who are in danger of
perishing eternally.

14th. Recommend yourself often
to those whom you know to be the
friends of God, that they may teach
you how act, and how to advance in
his love.

15th. From time to time, to humble
yourself in the eyes of others, ask to
fill some office more lowly than usual.
This practice serves wonderfully to
acquire an absolute empire over ourselves and our actions, and an interior contempt of the world.

16th. Perform, occasionally, some
public mortification.

17th. Let sweetness and benignity distill from your lips. O! how do sweet and gentle words edify our neighbor!—how much do they excite to love of God.

18th. Above all things, be firm in your resolution, not to refuse any thing to our Lord which you know He requires of you, and the performance of which will please Him. Say to Him often: Lord, look down upon me, watch over all my actions, my thoughts, &c. In every thing, and in all times, I wish to be thine, cost what it will. Say what thou desirest to me: I am resolved to do it, with the succor of thy holy grace, and under the powerful protection of thy beloved mother. Whoever has not this determined and absolute will, can only have a weak, imperfect love.

DEVOTIONS

IN HONOR OF THE

SACRED HEART OF JESUS.

Make His works known among the people—shew
this forth in all the earth.—Isaias xii, 4,5.

OBSERVATIONS.

THIS practice, in honor of the Sacred Heart of Jesus, plain in itself,
but filled with the spirit of true
piety, is divided into nine different
offices, taken from the heavenly
lights, which our Lord communicated
to his servant, the Ven. Marguerite
Mary Alacoque, a religious of the
Order of the Visitation. It embraces
whatever is most glorious to the Sacred Heart of Jesus. By this practice, without over-burdening any one

with vocal prayers or exterior practices, we may pay to this Divine Heart a continual, interior adoration, distributed among many, which any single person, howsoever fervent, would not be able to perform.

For this purpose, it is convenient to make the following observations:

1st. On the Thursday preceding the first Friday of every month, the nine offices of which this devotion consists, will be distributed to those consecrated to the Sacred Heart, and each will endeavor to acquit himself of this office with all possible exactness until the next month.

2d. The first Friday of every month is to be distinguished from the rest by the fervor with which all our actions ought to be animated. Therefore—as our Saviour enjoined to the Ven. Marg. Mary, in her life, written by Mr. Languet, (Book 4,) all will receive the Holy Communion with the leave of their respective Superior or Spiritual Director, and renew the act of consecration.

3d. Every one, for the better performance of his office, will strive in all the services he shall render to the Sacred Heart, to unite himself to the choir of blessed Spirits indicated in the Office itself, and make with them that mystical association which the Ven. Marguerite made with so great a profit to her soul, (Book V, of her life,) in order that they may supply our deficiencies, and fill our places in the hours of sleep, and at all other times, whatever may be our impediments: thus the Sacred Heart will be perpetually adored.

4th. And because the purest Heart of MARY is, after the Sacred Heart of Jesus, the most amiable and lovely, and bears the greatest resemblance to it, all the associates will cherish a tender devotion to this Sovereign

Queen, honoring Her to their utmost, especially on her principal feasts, and on the first Saturday of every month; joining their actions and affections to those of this immaculate Virgin in all the pious acts which they may exhibit to the Divine Heart; for it is the most efficacious way to preserve and spread the devotion to the Sacred Heart of Jesus.

5th. The greatest service which all have to present to the most Sacred Heart of Jesus, and the chief fruit to be proposed or intended in the execution of this pious exercise, is the exact observance of all our rules, and duties of our state; bearing constantly in mind the words of Jesus Christ to the Ven. Marg. Mary: "Thou canst not do anything more agreeable to to me than to run on with a constant fidelity and sincerity in the way of thy rules, in which the least defects are great in my sight; a religious person deceives himself, and withdraws far from me, when he thinks to please me without the exact observance of his rules."

6th. To connect more strictly the bond of Charity, which unites in the Sacred Heart of Jesus those that practice this devotion, each of them will pray every day for his companions, asking of the Sacred Heart that its love may be increased in all, and that none become cold, or withdraw themselves from this happy union. For this purpose it will be expedient to encourage one another, and propagate, by every means in their power, the reign of the Sacred Heart.

7th. When any one has to separate from his companions, he will not thereby cease to belong to this pious union of special worshipers of the divine Heart, provided he perseveres in performing the spiritual exercises.

8th. To avoid all scruples, it is to

be observed, that whatever has been said, either in respect to the nine Offices, or to the foregoing acts or exercises, is always and in every circumstance, understood not to be binding. The love of the Sacred Heart alone, and the close band of this sweet union, are the end and motive of whatever is proposed.

The Ven. Marg. Mary, addressing a letter, dated the 10th of August, 1589, to a Religious of the Society of Jesus, on the happiness of those persons who, at that time, had already embraced this devotion, writes thus: O! what great favor has God bestowed upon these souls, by granting them so early to taste of a devotion which is so fit to sanctify them! I see all of them in this Divine Heart elected and predestined to love him eternally. But it is for the Reverend Father of the Society of Jesus, that Jesus has reserved the grace to make

known the value of this precious
treasure, from which, the more we
draw the more it becomes abundant.
They then have it in their power to
enrich themselves with all kinds of
spiritual goods, and with the most
efficacious graces to discharge their
duties with the perfection they desire.
This Divine Heart will impart to their
sermons, in so great an abundance,
the sweet unction of Charity, that
with them, as with a two-edged
sword, they will pierce the most
hardened hearts, drawing the most
obstinate sinners to repentance.
Lastly, our Lord has resolved to dif-
fuse by this means the abundance of
his divine treasures of grace and
salvation upon the Order of the
Visitation and the Society of Jesus,
demanding in return from both religious Orders, a continual homage
of love, honor, and praise, and an
incessant vigilance in establishing

and propagating His kingdom in the hearts of all. But the Lord expects from your Society especially great things on this point, and the designs which He has on it are very great.

O. A. M. D. G.

FIRST OFFICE.

PROMOTER.

TRULY happy shall he be, to whose lot this office may have fallen, because our loving Saviour has said, "He would Himself be Mediator between Him and His Divine Father." The Promoter then shall beg of the Eternal Father, to enlighten all men, that they may know the Sacred Heart of Jesus; He will beg of the Holy Ghost, to make our hearts earnest in loving; and of the Blessed Virgin, that she would employ her

intercession to obtain, that the influence of this Divine Heart may be ex-
perienced by all who implore its
mercy. To fulfil this office, be faithful in the following PRACTICES :

1. Communicate on the first Friday of the
month, or on the Sunday following.

2. Visit, at least once a day, the Blessed Sacrament of the Altar, in union with the Choir of
Thrones, and say—

O august Choir of Thrones, I
unite myself to you, that in your
company I may honor the Sacred
Heart of Jesus.

O holy Mary! Mother of my Lord!
obtain for me, that I may love His
Sacred Heart.

O my amiable Jesus, grant, through
thy infinite goodness, that all men
may know the unparalleled excel-
lence of thy Sacred Heart ; and that
having trampled under foot the
world's deceitful pleasures, they may
taste the unalterable delights which

thou hast prepared for those who sincerely love thee. Amen.

3. Our Father. Hail Mary. Creed.

O sweetest Heart of Jesus, I implore that I may ever love thee, more and more.

Recite also, the daily prayers to the Most Holy Trinity, and to the Blessed Virgin—p. 127, 128.

N. B. The above prayers can be all said during the holy sacrifice of the Mass; and this remark applies to all the similar prayers that follow.

SECOND OFFICE.

REPAIRER.

THE Repairer shall (in compliance with the wish of our Lord) most humbly beg pardon of God for the injuries which are offered to Him in the most holy Sacrament of the Altar; and he may rest assured that our Lord will more and more forgive him the

punishment due to his sins, and will
make him enjoy the sweet effects of
his mercy. To fulfil this office, be
faithful in the following Practices:

1. Communicate on the first Friday of the
month, or on the Sunday following.

2. Renew every Friday the Act of Reparation
to the Sacred Heart of Jesus.

3. Visit every day the most Blessed Sacrament,
in union with the Choir of Powers, and say—

August Choir of Heavenly Powers,
come to my assistance, that I may be
able to make some atonement for the
many outrages the Sacred Heart receives in the Blessed Sacrament.

O holy Mary! Mother of my Lord!
obtain for me, that I may love His
Sacred Heart.

O my Jesus! I desire to shut myself up within the wound of thy Sacred Heart, that I may never more be
separated from thee. I desire. O my
good Lord, to employ every possible
means to atone for the many offences
that are offered thee; and through

love to thy most adorable Heart, I
desire to yield up my last breath in
thy service.   O my God! I offer this
Sacred Heart to thy Divine Majesty,
in satisfaction for the many outrages
thou continually receivest from
sinners.

4. Our Father. Hail Mary. Creed.

O sweetest Heart of Jesus, I implore, that I may ever love thee more
and more.

THIRD OFFICE.

ADORER.

OFTEN retire in spirit into the Heart
of Jesus, to adore Him and to love
Him with all your strength.   Rejoice
in the eternal praises of God, saying
with the Angels, "Holy! holy! holy!
is the Lord God Almighty."   Be
faithful also in the following Practices:

1. Communicate on the first Friday **of the** month, or on the Sunday following.

2. Every day, make a visit to our Lord, in the Blessed Eucharist, in union with the Choir of Dominations, and say—

O exalted choir of the Heavenly Dominations, offer with me to the august Heart of Jesus, all the good that is done throughout the Catholic world, and consecrate it to His greater glory.

O holy Mary! Mother of my Lord! obtain for me, that I may love His Sacred Heart.

O my Jesus, worthy Adorer of the Divine Majesty, I join myself with my whole soul to the adorations which thou dost render to thy Heavenly Father in the secrecy of thy Divine Heart ; and I fervently wish that all the faith and love with which thou inspirest the most blessed Virgin Mary and thy Saints, could be contained in mine, in order to honor and glorify thee, now and forever, in proportion to thy merits.   Amen.

4. Our Father. Hail Mary. Creed.

O sweetest Heart of Jesus, I implore, that I may ever love thee more and more.

FOURTH OFFICE.

LOVING SERVANT.

"The Heart of Jesus wishes all things to be done through love. Let us then love Him without reserve ; let us give and sacrifice every thing to obtain the love of Jesus; if we possess the Heart of God, we shall have all things." To fulfil this sublime office then, be faithful in the following Practices:

1. Communicate on the first Friday of the month, or on the Sunday following.

2. Visit, at least once a day, our loving Lord in the Blessed Sacrament, in union with the Choir of Seraphim, and say—

Ye Blessed Seraphim of Paradise! obtain for me that burning love of the Sacred Heart of Jesus, with which you are continually inflamed, and let your ceaseless adorations compensate for our great coldness and indifference.

O holy Mary! Mother of my Lord! obtain for me, that I may love his Sacred Heart.

O most holy Heart of my Jesus, burning furnace of that divine love, which thou camest to enkindle in the hearts of all men, consume my heart with these heavenly flames, that it may love thee alone. Ye, Seraphim of the Celestial Court, I beseech you to present to the author of my being, my ardent desire that my heart may be enflamed with love for Him. Amen.

3. Our Father. Hail Mary. Creed.

O sweetest Heart of Jesus, I implore, that I may ever love thee more and more.

FIFTH OFFICE.

DISCIPLE.

You can do nothing better calculated to make you a true disciple of Christ than to imitate his meekness and humility. Such is the lesson He himself points out for our study, when he says: "Learn of me, for I am meek and humble of heart." Endeavor then to model your life upon this perfect pattern of meekness and humility. The duties of this office will be fulfilled by a faithful compliance with the following Practices:

1. Communicate on the first Friday of the month, or on the Sunday following.

2. Visit your meek Saviour in the Blessed Eucharist, at least once a day, in union with the Choir of Cherubim, and say—

Ye holy Cherubim! receive me into your company, that I may be witness of the heavenly splendor which proceeds from the most Sacred Heart of my Jesus.

O holy Mary! Mother of my Lord! obtain for me, that I may love His Sacred Heart.

He very shortly will be learned, whom thou, O Divine Heart, undertakest to teach. Ah! teach me also, O amiable Heart; and since thou hast been so good as to appoint me thy Disciple, grant that my heart may be docile to thy divine lessons, and do thou convert all those who are opposed to truth. Amen.

3. Our Father. Hail Mary. Creed.

O sweetest Heart of Jesus, I implore, that I may ever love thee more and more.

SIXTH OFFICE.

VICTIM.

" Jesus in the blessed Sacrament is like the victim of God, and the fire of divine love would consume Him, were He not immortal and impassible." Offer yourself to the Eternal Father, together with the Heart of Jesus, especially during Mass and Communion, to obtain more easily the divine mercy for poor sinners : be faithful also in the following Practices :

1. Communicate on the first Friday of the month, or on the Sunday following.

2. Visit daily our amiable Saviour in the Blessed Eucharist, in union with the Choir of Virtues, and say—

With you, O holy Choir of Virtues ! do I adore the divine justice to which the most loving Heart of Jesus was sacrificed in atonement for our sins.

O holy Mary! Mother of my Lord! obtain for me, that I may love His Sacred Heart.

O most Holy Heart, who, upon our altars, makest thyself a Victim of love, what dost thou desire, what dost thou seek, but victims to continue in them thy sacrifice? Behold me here, O Lord! take possession of me, that I may be a victim sacrificed and consumed in the flames of thy love, for the greater glory of the Eternal Father and for the salvation of sinners. O Heavenly Father, who hast chosen me as a victim, be pleased to accept me through the Sacred Heart of thy only Son, sacrificed for me. Amen.

3. Our Father. Hail Mary. Creed.

O sweetest Heart of Jesus, I implore, that I may ever love thee more and more.

SEVENTH OFFICE.

FAITHFUL SERVANT.

" You will sacrifice yourself to the Sacred Heart of Jesus, so as to will nothing but according to His holy will." Therefore, again and again offer up your heart to Jesus as to your Master and Lord, by the words: " O Lord! I am thy servant," and by preferring in every thing His most holy will to your own. To fulfil this office, be faithful in the following Practices:

1. Communicate on the first Friday of the month, or on the Sunday following.

2. Visit daily your good Master in the Holy Eucharist, uniting yourself with the Archangels, and saying—

O holy choir of Archangels, call together those that are invited to the table of the divine Lamb, and adorn them with the nuptial garment.

O holy Mary! Mother of my Lord!

obtain for me, that I may love His Sacred Heart.

O omnipotent love of my God who hast broken the chains that restrained me far from thee. O! woul! that I could persuade all those wl. wander as I did, to taste at thy Altars, the delights of this new service, which renders happy all those that embrace it. O mysterious subjection of Jesus in the sacrament of His love, I devote myself entirely to honor thee, and to seek, or to desire at least, that every heart may be turned to thee. Amen.

3. Our Father. Hail Mary. Creed.

O sweetest Heart of Jesus, I implore, that I may ever love thee more and more.

EIGHTH OFFICE.

SUPPLIANT.

" OUR Lord has promised that he
will be favorable in their last moments to those, who, animated with
the disposition of the Blessed Virgin
on Mount Calvary, will come every
Friday and adore Him on the cross;
offering this holy disposition to the
Eternal Father, with the sufferings
of his Son, to obtain the conversion
of all hardened and unfaithful hearts.
Adopt then a devotion so pleasing to
the Sacred Heart, and be faithful also
in the following Practices :

1. Communicate on the first Friday of the
month, or on the Sunday following.

2. Visit daily our dear Saviour in the Blessed
Eucharist, in union with the holy Choir of Angels,
and say—

O amiable Choir of Angels, and
you in particular, dear Guardian
Angels accompany me in this visit

to our Lord, and offer the Sacred Heart of Jesus to the Eternal Father, together with all my prayers, actions and sufferings for his greater glory, and for the repose of the souls in Purgatory.

O holy Mary! Mother of my God! obtain for me, that I may love His Sacred Heart.

O Divine Heart! hear the cries of the needy, and be the consoler of the afflicted, since thou hast always been pleased, O merciful Heart! to forgive and to do good to all.   Amen.

3. Our Father. Hail Mary. Creed.

O sweetest Heart of Jesus, I implore, that I may ever love thee more and more.

4. Pray every day for the agonizing and for the repose of the poor souls in Purgatory.

NINTH OFFICE.

ZEALOUS.

"Our Lord has made known to me, (said the Ven. Marg. Mary,) that several names are written in His Heart, on account of the desire they have of causing it to be honored; and that these names he will never permit to be erased. Therefore, the zealous for the salvation of others, shall take special care in procuring the glory of the Sacred Heart of Jesus by word and example, and by fidelity to the following Practices:

1. Communicate on the first Friday of the month, or on the Sunday following.

2. Visit daily our Divine Redeemer in the Blessed Eucharist, in union with the Choir of Principalities, and say—

O Zealous Spirits! Principalities of Heaven! offer yourselves in union with all the other angelic hosts of the Divine Majesty, and obtain through

your intercession that the Sacred
Heart of my Jesus may be known
throughout the whole world, and
that he may draw to his love, the
numberless idolaters and infidels,
who know him not, and the many
ungrateful Christians who refuse to
pay Him that tribute of honor and
adoration which He deserves.

O holy Mary! Mother of my Lord!
obtain for me, that I may love His
Sacred Heart.

O Sacred Heart of Jesus, who
lovest us so tenderly, how amiable
thou art! When shall I see thee
ardently loved by all! O! that I
could spread abroad the wonders of
thy love, and obtain from every heart
a faithful correspondence to it. Amen.

3. Our Father. Hail Mary. Creed.

O sweetest Heart of Jesus, I implore, that I may ever love thee more
and more.

Recite also, the daily prayers to the Most Holy Trinity, and to the Blessed Virgin.

N. B. The above prayers can be all said during the holy Sacrifice of the Mass.

A PRAYER,

To be said daily by all the members.

O Most Holy Trinity, one God! I offer to Thee, in union with the merits of our Lord Jesus Christ, all my prayers, actions and sufferings of this day for Thy greater glory and the accomplishment of Thy holy will : in honor of the Blessed Virgin Mary; my holy Angel Guardian, and all my patron Saints; for the propagation of the devotion to the Sacred Heart of Jesus and Mary; in full remission and satisfaction for my sins; for the conversion of sinners and the perseverance of the just: for the repose of

the souls in purgatory; for the
spiritual profit and perfection of the
members of our Confraternity, and
for all those for whom I am bound to
pray; also, in thanksgiving for all
the graces which Thou hast hitherto
conferred on me, or which Thou wilt
hereafter bestow on me, through the
merits of Jesus Christ, our Lord.
Amen.

PRAYER TO THE B. V. MARY.

To be said every day by all the members.

O, MY Queen! O, my Mother! I
offer myself entirely to thee, and as
a proof of my devotion, I consecrate
to thee, this day, my sight, my hear-
ing, my speech, my heart, my whole
person.

Since, therefore, I am thine, O
gracious mother! preserve me, defend

me, as thy property and thy possession. Amen.

ASPIRATIONS IN EVERY TEMPTATION.

O! Mary! O! my Mother! remember that I am thine. Preserve me,
defend me, as thy property and thy
possession.

AN ACT OF ATONEMENT

(EVERY FRIDAY,)

TO THE SACRED HEART OF JESUS.

O! Adorable Heart of my Saviour
and my God, penetrated with a lively
sorrow at the sight of the outrages
which Thou hast received, and which
Thou daily dost receive in the Sacrament of Thy love, behold me prostrate at the foot of Thy altar, to
make an acceptable atonement. O!
that I were able, by my homage and

veneration, to make satisfaction to
Thine injured honor, and efface with
my tears and with my blood, so
many irreverences, profanations, and
sacrileges which outrage Thine infinite
goodness.   How well should my life
be disposed of, could it be sacrificed
for so worthy an object!   Pardon,
Divine Saviour, my ingratitude, and
all the infidelities and indignities
which I myself have committed
against Thy Sovereign Majesty. Remember that Thy adorable Heart,
bearing the weight of my sins in the
days of its mortal life, was sorowful
even unto death; do not suffer Thy
agony and Thy blood to be unprofitable to me.   Annihilate within me
my criminal heart, and give me one
according to Thine—a heart contrite
and humble, a heart pure and spot-
less, a heart which may be henceforth a victim consecrated to Thy
glory, and inflamed with the sacred

fire of Thy love. O! Lord, I deplore
in the bitterness of my heart, my
former irreverences and sacrileges,
which I wish in future to repair, by
my pious deportment in the churches,
my assiduity in visiting and my devotion and fervor in receiving the
most holy Sacrament of the altar.
But in order to render my respect
and my adoration more grateful to
Thee, I unite them with those which
are rendered to Thee in our temples,
by those blessed spirits who are at
the foot of Thy sacred tabernacles.
Hear their vows, O! my God, and
accept the homages of a heart which
returns to Thee with the sole view of
loving only Thee, that I may merit
to love thee eternally.   Amen.

AN ACT OF CONSECRATION.

(FOR THE FIRST FRIDAY OF THE MONTH,)

TO THE ADORABLE HEART OF JESUS.

I GIVE and consecrate to the Adorable Heart of Jesus my being, my life, my thoughts, my words, my actions, my pains, and my sufferings. I wish for life only, that my days may be employed in loving, honoring and adoring it. I take Thee, then, O! Divine Heart, for the object of my love, the protector of my life, the assurance of my salvation, the remedy of my inconstancy, the repairer of all my defects, and my certain asylum at the hour of my death. O! Heart, abounding in mercy, turn from me the arrows of the just wrath of the Father. I place all my confidence in Thee; for I fear every thing from my weakness, as I hope for every thing from Thy goodness. Destroy in me every thing which may displease and resist Thee; implant so deeply Thy love in my heart that I may never forget Thee, nor be separated from Thee. I conjure Thee by Thy infinite goodness, to transform me into a victim entirely consecrated to Thy glory, which may be from this moment inflamed, and one day consumed in the fire of Thy love. This is the only object of my desires, having no other ambition than that of living and dying in Thee and for Thee. Amen.

MAY the Divine Heart of Jesus, and the immaculate heart of Mary be forever praised, blessed, loved, served and glorified by men and Angels. Amen.

ACTS OF ADORATION.

"THE ensuing four and twenty acts of adoration to Jesus Christ in the blessed Sacrament, may be recited by way of reparation for all the offences committed against him by mankind."

1. Jesus, our Lord and our God, ever adorable! O! that we could be present in all the churches throughout the universe, where thou art not adored as thou oughtest to be, and where thy inflamed love is not repaid with a gratitude worthy thy Majesty! We fly at least in spirit, to these holy places now profaned, and offer on Thy altars there, the fervent love and adoration of thy holy Mother, in compensation for the injuries ever done thee by the Jews, by heretics, and bad Christians. *Eternal praise*

be to the ever blessed Sacrament of the Altar.

2. O Jesus! true Sun, that dost enlighten the Church, and raisest into a flame the hearts of thy servants! we adore thee, and to repair the sloth, indifference, and tepidity, of so many religious persons, who, though favored with the aspect of so burning a luminary, remain cold, insensible, and inanimate, we offer up to thee, all the inflamed desires of the Seraphim. *Eternal praise, &c.*

3. We adore thee, O eternal wisdom! and to repair the gross ignorance which has caused us to offend thee, we offer up to thee all the knowledge of those most enlightened spirits, the Cherubim. *Eternal praise, &c.*

4. We adore thee, O most meek and merciful God! and to repair all the sins of anger, passion, and revenge, highly offensive in thy sight,

wo offer up to thee the peace, mild-
ness, and tranquillity of the Thrones.
Eternal praise, &c.

5. We adore thee, O Sacrament of
of Love! and to repair all the thoughts
and criminal desires conceived even
at the foot of thy altars, we offer up
to thee all the pure affections and
chaste desires of the Dominations.
Eternal praise, &c.

6. We adore thee, O immaculate
Lamb! that takest away the sins of
the world! and to repair all the irreverences, gazing at dangerous objects and disrespectful postures during the time of holy Mass, we offer up
to thee the profound respect of the
Choir of Virtues. *Eternal praise, &c.*

7. We adore thee, O source and
origin of all sanctity and innocence!
and to repair the abominations committed by wicked priests, who consecrate and receive thee in the state of
mortal sin: we offer up to thee the

profound adoration and holiness of the Powers. *Eternal praise, &c.*

8. We adore thee, sovereign Lord of the universe! to whom all knees both in heaven and earth should bend, and all reverence be paid; and in order to repair the many blasphemies against thy honor, we offer up to thee the praises and homage of the Principalities. *Eternal praise, &c.*

9. We adore thee, Saviour of the world! to whom all fidelity and glory is due, and to repair the sacrilegious communions and treacheries of so many false consciences, we offer up to thee the fervent and faithful zeal of the Archangels. *Eternal praise, &c.*

10. We adore thee, the delight of heaven and earth! and to repair the neglect, indifference, and contempt mankind shows to that amorous invitation by which thou callest them to thy sweet embraces in the holy Eu-

charist, we offer up to thee the ready obedience, content and happiness of the Angels. *Eternal praise, &c.*

11. We adore thee, never failing bounty and goodness! and to repair man's offensive diffidence in thy tender mercy, we offer up to thee the steadfast reliance and assurance of the holy Patriarchs in thy promises. *Eternal praise, &c.*

12. We adore thee, O amiable Jesus! and revere the sacred mystery of the blessed Eucharist, revealed by thy Divine word, taught by the Church, and proved by miracles; and to repair the doubts men have had of thy real presence in the holy Sacrament, we offer up to thee the due submission shown by the Prophets to thy Divine oracles. *Eternal praise, &c.*

13. We adore thee, most tender and most amiable of all Fathers! and to make reparation for the errors

and infidelities of thy own children, we offer up to thee the faith of the Apostles. *Eternal praise, &c.*

14. We adore thee, most loving Shepherd, pattern of true charity! and to make reparation for the designs, of revenge conceived in defiance of thy Divine prohibitions, we offer up to thee, the patience and prayers of the Martyrs in favor of their persecutors. *Eternal praise, &c.*

15. We adore thee, inexhaustible fund of treasures! and to make reparation for all the robberies committed in thy churches, we offer up to thee the rich and bountiful donations of thy devout servants. *Eternal praise, &c.*

16. We adore thee, O most watchful advocate! and to make reparation for the many negligences of those who have any authority in the Church to correct the abuses and irreverences

there committed against thee, we offer up to thee the exact attention and careful solicitude of holy Bishops and Prelates. *Eternal praise, &c.*

17. We adore thee, O God of infinite majesty! whom we can never sufficiently adore and reverence; and to make reparation for all the impious oaths pronounced against thee, we offer up to thee the pious discourses made in thy honor by the holy Doctors of the Church. *Eternal praise, &c.*

18. We adore thee, most hidden and most humble Divinity! and to make reparation for all the contests, disputes, punctilios of honor and scandal, by which thou hast been offended, we offer up to thee the humility of the holy Confessors. *Eternal praise, &c.*

19. We adore thee, eternal Priest! whose delight is to offer sacrifice! and to make reparation for the in-

sults and affronts done to thy Priests, Religious, and Virgins, we offer up to thee thy own invincible patience, together with the true and fervent zeal of all good Priests and Apostolic Preachers. *Eternal praise, &c.*

20. We adore thee, true bread of Angels! and to make reparation for the sins committed against thy command of abstinence, we offer up to thee the fasts and temperance of the holy Anchorets. *Eternal praise, &c.*

21. We adore thee, O God of all purity! and to make reparation for all the sins which have hitherto been committed against the virtue of purity, we offer up to thee the modesty and penance of all holy religious men and women. *Eternal praise, &c.*

22. We adore thee, amiable spouse of our souls! and to make reparation for all the lukewarmness and indifference shown by many, particularly in time of holy Communion, we offer

up to thee the raptures and ecstacies of holy Virgins. *Eternal praise, &c.*

23. We adore thee, most worthy object of the love and affection of men and angels! and to repair the profanations committed in thy churches by the effusion of so much innocent blood, as also to make some atonement for the poor and indigent manner in which thou art entertained there, we offer up to thee the piety of all the blessed saints, and the distress and want in which thy persecuted servants lived. *Eternal praise, &c.*

24. We adore thee, Son of the ever glorious Virgin! and to make a general reparation, as much as lies in our power, for all the indignities thou hast suffered from men since the institution of this adorable mystery, we have recourse to thy holy Mother; looking upon her, as under thee, the

greatest and most secure refuge of sinners. *Eternal praise, &c.*

O Queen of heaven and earth! hope of mankind, who adorest thy Divine Son incessantly, we entreat thee, that since we have the honor to be of the number of thy children, thou wouldst interest thyself in our behalf, and make satisfaction for us, and in our name, to our eternal Judge, by rendering to him the duties we ourselves are incapable of performing. Amen.

"It would be advisable to recite these acts every Thursday or Friday. Their number corresponds to the hours of the day and night. In each of these hours, the most amiable Heart of Jesus in the Eucharist is offended and insulted throughout the world. This recital of the above acts, is a reparation of honor we make for these offences: nor can it seem too much. However,

if on account of other occupations it
should appear so, fail not once a
month at least, and particularly on
the Feast of the Sacred Heart, to acquit yourself of this duty. You
will let me, devout soul, recommend
to your piety another most easy
practice. You have, perhaps, a
number of friends, and those equally
engaged with you in this holy devotion. Take to yourself one of these
acts, divide the others amongst your
friends. Let each of them recite
daily and offer up to God his respective adoration. Nothing can be more
practicable, nothing more agreeable
to the amiable and offended Heart of
your Divine Saviour, or more satis-
factory, for so many offences, daily
committed against him.''

INDULGENCES

The Sacred Heart of Jesus.

REMARK 1.—There are two indispensable requisites to gain any Indulgence whatever. The first is, to be in the state of grace; the second, to comply with the conditions upon which it is granted.

REMARK 2.—A general condition to gain any of the Indulgences enumerated below, is, that the members of the Confraternity shall recite daily, in honor of the Sacred Heart of Jesus, the Lord's Prayer, the Hail Mary, the Creed, and the short Aspiration: "Benign Heart of Jesus! grant that I may love thee more and more." The other conditions will be indicated in the notes, page 154.

REMARK 3.—When the visit of a church is required by the conditions of the Indulgence, the members who could not make this visit are to perform some other pious work enjoined by their Confessor.

A PLENARY INDULGENCE:—1st. On the day of admission into the Confraternity. (A)

2d. On the first Friday, or the first Sunday of every month. (A)

145

3d. Once a month, on any day, at the choice of the members. (A)

4th. Once a month, for those who recite three times, *Glory be to the Father,* &c., morning, afternoon, and night, in thanksgiving to the Most Holy Trinity, for the graces and privileges bestowed on the Blessed Virgin Mary, especially in her glorious Assumption. (A) Also, an Indulgence of one hundred days for each recitation.

5th. At the hour of death for those who, being truly penitent and resigned to the Divine Will, invoke at least, from their heart, the Most Holy Name of Jesus.

An Indulgence of sixty days for every good work devoutly performed by the members of the Confraternity.

An indulgence of ten years and ten *quarantines* (that is, ten times forty days) on each of the three Ember days of the four seasons of the year. (B)

On the first of January, the Circumcision of our Lord, an indulgence of thirty years and thirty quarantines. (B)

On the 6th, the Epiphany, the same indulgence. (B)

On the 2d of February, the Purification of the Blessed Virgin Mary, a plenary indulgence. (c)

On the 24th, St. Mathias, an indulgence of seven years and seven quarantines. (B)

On Septuagesima, Sexigesima, and Quinquagesima Sundays, an indulgence of thirty years and thirty quarantines. (B)

On Ash Wednesday, an indulgence of fifteen years and fifteen quarantines. (B)

On the fourth Sunday in Lent, the same indulgence. (B)

On Palm Sunday, an indulgence of twenty-five years and twenty-five quarantines. (B)

On Holy Thursday, a plenary in·dulgence. (c)

On Good Friday, an indulgence of thirty years and thirty quarantines. (B)

On Holy Saturday, the same indulgence. (B)

On every day in Lent, except those already mentioned, an indulgence of ten years and ten quarantines. (B)

On Easter Sunday, a plenary indulgence. (c)

Every day within the Octave of Easter, including Low Sunday, an indulgence of thirty years and thirty quarantines. (B)

On the 19th of March, St. Joseph's day, a plenary indulgence. (c)

On the 25th, the Annunciation of the Blessed Virgin Mary, the same indulgence. (c)

A plenary indulgence on each of the six Fridays, or the six Sundays, immediately preceding the Feast of the Sacred Heart. (D)

An indulgence of seven years and seven quarantines on each of the four Sundays immediately preceding the Feast of the Sacred Heart.

An indulgence of seven years and seven quarantines every day during the Novena which precedes the Feast of the Sacred Heart. (E)

An indulgence of seven years and seven quarantines on each of the three days immediately preceding the Feast of the Sacred Heart. (E)

A plenary indulgence on the Feast of the Sacred Heart of Jesus, or the Sunday following. (A)

On the 25th of April, St. Mark's day, an indulgence of thirty years and thirty quarantines. (B)

On each of the three Rogation days, the same indulgence. (B)

On Ascension Day, a plenary indulgence. (c)

On the Eve of Whit Sunday, an indulgence of ten years and ten quarantines. (B)

On Whit Sunday, and every day during the Octave until Saturday inclusively, an indulgence of thirty years and thirty quarantines. (B)

On the 1st of May, St. Philip and St. James, an indulgence of seven years and seven quarantines. (B)

On the 11th of June, St. Barnabas, an indulgence of seven years and seven quarantines. (B)

On the 29th, St. Peter and St. Paul, a plenary indulgence. (c)

On the 2d of July, the Visitation of the Blessed Virgin Mary, an indulgence of seven years and seven quarantines. (B)

On the 25th, St. James, an indulgence of seven years and seven quarantines. (B)

On the 15th of August, the Assumption of the Blessed Virgin Mary, a plenary indulgence. (c)

On the 24th, St. Bartholomew, an indulgence of seven years and seven quarantines. (B)

On the 8th of September, the Nativity of the Blessed Virgin Mary, a plenary indulgence. (c)

On the 21st, St. Matthew, an indulgence of seven years and seven quarantines. (B)

On the 28th of October, St. Simon and St. Jude, an indulgence of seven years and seven quarantines. (B)

On the 1st of November, All Saints, a plenary indulgence. (c)

On the 2d, the Commemoration of All Souls, a plenary indulgence. (c)

On the 21st, the Presentation of the Blessed Virgin Mary, an indulgence of seven years and seven quarantines. (B)

On the 30th, St. Andrew, the same indulgence. (B)

On the first and second Sundays of Advent, an indulgence of ten years and ten quarantines. (B)

On the third Sunday, an indulgence of fifteen years and fifteen quarantines. (B)

On the fourth Sunday, an indulgence of ten years and ten quarantines. (B)

On the 8th of December, the Conception of the Blessed Virgin Mary, a plenary indulgence. (c)

On the 21st, St. Thomas, an indulgence of seven years and seven quarantines. (B)

On the 24th, Christmas Eve, an indulgence of fifteen years and fifteen quarantines. (B)

On the 25th, Christmas day, a plenary indulgence (c), and also an indulgence of fifteen years and fifteen quarantines at the mid-night Mass, and at the second Mass at day-break. (B)

On the 26th, St. Stephen's day, an indulgence of thirty years and thirty quarantines. (B)

On the 27th, St. John, the same indulgence. (B)

On the 28th, the Holy Innocents, the same indulgence. (B)

All these Indulgences are applicable to the Souls in Purgatory.

NOTES.

(A) The conditions are, confession, communion, and prayers, according to the intention of the Pope.

(B) To gain this Indulgence, the members are to visit the church of their Confraternity, and there pray, according to the intention of the Pope.

(C) The conditions are, confession, communion, to visit the church of the Confraternity, and there pray, according to the intention of the Pope.

(D) The conditions are, confession, communion, to visit any church in which the Feast of the Sacred Heart is celebrated, and there pray, according to the intention of the Pope.

(E) To gain this Indulgence, the members are to visit the church in which the Feast of the Sacred Heart is celebrated, and there pray, according to the intention of the Pope.

PRAYERS

TO THE

SACRED HEART OF JESUS.

PRAYERS.*

WITH THREE OUR FATHER, &C.

"The Word was made flesh, and dwelt among us."

O ETERNAL Word, made man for the love of us! humbly prostrate at thy feet, we adore thee with the most profound respect, and to make reparation for our ingratitude in regard to so great a benefit, we unite in heart with all those who love thee, and offer thee our most humble and most sincere thanks. Feelingly impressed

---

* A plenary Indulgence, once a month, is attached to the daily recitation of these prayers, (see note A,) and an Indulgence of three hundred days, once a day.

155

with the exceedingly great humility,
goodness, and meekness, which we
behold in thy Divine Heart, we humbly beg the assistance of thy grace to
imitate these virtues, which are so
dear to thee. Our Father, &c. Hail
Mary, &c. Glory be, &c.

"He was also crucified, suffered under Pontius
Pilate, and was buried."

O JESUS, our amiable Redeemer!
humbly prostrate at thy feet, we
adore thee with the most profound
respect, and to give thee a proof of
the sorrow which we feel for our in-
sensibility to all the outrages which
thy loving Heart prompted thee to
suffer for our salvation, during thy
bitter Passion and death, we unite
with all those who love thee to give
thee thanks with our whole soul.
We admire the infinite patience and
generosity of thy Divine Heart, and
humbly beseech thee to fill ours with

that spirit of Christian mortification which will enable us courageously to bear sufferings, and place our greatest consolation and all our glory in thy Cross. Our Father, &c. Hail Mary, &c. Glory be, &c.

"Thou gavest them bread from heaven, having in it all that is delicious."

O JESUS, burning with love for us! humbly prostrate at thy sacred feet, we adore thee with the most profound respect, and in satisfaction for the outrages which thy Divine Heart daily receives in the most Holy Sacrament of the altar, we unite with all those who love thee, and are most thankful for thy benefits. We love in thy Divine Heart that incomprehensible fire of charity with which it is inflamed for thy Eternal Father, and we beseech thee to kindle in ours an ardent love for thee, and for our neighbor. Our Father, &c. Hail Mary, &c. Glory be, &c.

Finally, O most amiable Jesus! we beseech thee by the sweetness of thy Divine Heart, to convert sinners, to comfort the afflicted, to assist those who are in their agony, and to relieve the souls in Purgatory. Unite our hearts in the bond of true peace and charity; deliver us from an unprovided death, and grant that ours may be holy and undisturbed. Amen.

V. Heart of Jesus, burning with love for us!

R. Inflame our hearts with love for thee.

Let us pray.

GRANT we beseech thee, O Almighty God! that we who glory in the most holy Heart of thy beloved Son, and commemorate the principal benefits of his love towards us, may rejoice, not only in receiving them, but also in the fruit which they will produce in our souls. Through the same Jesus Christ, thy Son, our Lord.

O Divine Heart of Jesus! I adore thee with all the powers of my soul, and consecrate them for ever to thee, with all my thoughts, words, actions, and my whole being. I wish to offer thee acts of adoration, love, and praise, similar as much as possible to those which thou offerest to the Eternal Father. Be thou, I beseech thee, the repairer of my faults, the protector of my life, my refuge and security at the hour of my death. O most loving Jesus! through the anguish and bitter sorrows which thou didst endure for my sake during the whole course of thy mortal life, grant me perfect contrition for my sins, true contempt for earthly things, an ardent desire of eternal glory, a lively confidence in thy infinite mercies, and final perseverance in thy grace.

O most loving Heart of Jesus! I offer thee these humble prayers for myself, and for all those who unite with me to adore thee. Vouchsafe to receive them in thy infinite goodness and graciously to hear them, especially for him amongst us who will first depart this mortal life. Most benign Heart of my Saviour! pour into his soul, amid the agonies of death, thy inward consolations; receive him into thy sacred wounds, purify him from all earthly defilements in that furnace of love, that he may be admitted into the mansions of bliss, and become an intercessor with thee for all those who will still remain in this land of exile.

Most holy Heart of my amiable Jesus! I wish to renew these prayers and acts of adoration every time I breathe till the very last moment of my life, and to offer them to thee for myself, a miserable sinner, and for all who are associated to adore thee. I pray thee, O my Jesus! for the holy Church, thy beloved spouse and our true mother, for the just, for all sinners, for those who are in their agony, and for all mankind: let not the blood which was shed for their sake, prove useless to them; vouchsafe also to apply it to the relief of the souls in purgatory, and particularly to the souls of those who during their life, have practised the holy devotion of adoring thee.

Most amiable heart of Mary! which among the hearts of all creatures art the purest, the most inflamed with love for that of Jesus, and at the same time the most mericful towards sinners, obtain for us of our Divine Redeemer, the graces which we beg of thee. O mother of mercy! one aspiration, a mere motion of thy loving heart towards that of thy Divine Son, can procure entire consolation to our souls; do then intercede for us with him, and, moved by the filial love which he had and always will have for thee, he will infallibly grant our petitions.   Amen.

A DAILY OFFERING.*

O MY amiable Jesus! I, N. N., to testify my gratitude to thee and make reparation for all my infidelities, give thee my heart. I consecrate myself entirely to thee, and, with the assistance of thy grace, I firmly purpose to sin no more for the future.

---

* A plenary indulgence, once a month, is attached to the daily recitation of this prayer before an image of the Sacred Heart, (see note A,) and an indulgence of one hundred days, once a day.

A PRAYER TO THE B. SACRAMENT AND TO THE S. HEART.*

"He loved me, and delivered himself for me."

Gal. ii, 20.

BEHOLD how far thy infinite love has gone, O loving Jesus! out of thy sacred flesh and precious blood thou hast prepared a divine banquet to give thyself entirely to me. What could ever have prompted thee to such demonstrations of love? Nothing, undoubtedly, but thy most loving Heart. O adorable Heart of my Saviour! burning furnace of the divine love, receive my soul into thy sacred wound, that, at this school of Charity, I may learn to love that God who has given me such proofs of his love. Amen.

* An indulgence of one hundred days, once a day, is attached to the recitation of this prayer.

AN ACT OF CONSECRATION.

ADORABLE Heart of Jesus! in which "all the fullness of the Godhead dwelleth corporally!" penetrated with gratitude for thy unbounded mercies, I consecrate myself entirely to thee,—my body, my soul, my thoughts, my words, my actions, and all the affections of my heart. The remainder of my life shall be spent in thy service, sanctified by thy love, and devoted to thy glory. Thou wilt henceforth be my refuge in affliction, my light, my hope, my strength, my consolation, my all. Thy will shall be the rule of my life, and by following it, I shall walk in the paths of justice and peace. Bless, O Divine Jesus! and consume my sacrifice by the sacred fire of thy love. Annihilate in me all that is displeasing in thy sight. Render my heart like to

thine,—humble, meek, patient, and
pure. Hide it within thy own, that
it may never be separated from thee.
Amen.

AN ACT OF REPARATION.

ADORABLE Heart of Jesus, Victim
of propitiation for our sins! the contemplation of thy infinite goodness
for mankind, and of their ingratitude
towards thee, absorbs all the powers
of my soul. Always burning with
love for them in the Sacrament of
of our Altars, thou art daily offended
by their irreverences and sacrilegious
profanations. "Be astonished, O ye
heavens! at this: they have forgot-
ten the Lord, they have blasphemed
the Holy One of Israel!" Penetrated
with grief at the thought of these
enormities, I prostrate myself before
thee, O Divine Redeemer! to make
reparation for them by the most

humble and fervent acts of adoration.
" We have sinned, we have done un-
justly, we have committed wicked-
ness ;" but remember, O Jesus ! that
thy loving Heart bore the weight of
our iniquities in the days of thy
mortal life: it was wounded, it bled
for them on the Cross, and its last
aspiration was an appeal for mercy
and forgiveness in behalf of sinners.
Spare us then, O Jesus! spare thy
people, whom thou hast redeemed
with thy precious blood.   Accept the
tribute   of   praise   and   gratitude
which we offer for the infinite love
which   renders thee present in our
tabernacles; pardon our former trans-
gressions, and   bless the resolution
which we   now   take, of repairing
them by our respect and devotion in
thy divine presence, and particularly
by the fervor with which we will receive thee in Holy Communion.   Enkindle in our hearts the fire of thy

love, withdraw our affections from all earthly things, and mercifully grant that we may live in thee and for thee. Amen.

ASPIRATIONS TO THE S. HEART.

HEART of Jesus, in which "are hid all the treasures of wisdom and knowledge!" be thou my comfort in adversity, my guide in prosperity, and my protection against my enemies, visible and invisible.

Heart of Jesus, perfect adorer of the heavenly Father! teach me to adore Him with thee and by thee, in spirit and truth.

Heart of Jesus, Victim of propitiation! grant that I may truly repent and atone for my sins.

Heart of Jesus, consumed by the ardor of thy zeal for the glory of God! grant that I may seek it in all my actions.

Heart of Jesus, obedient unto death, and even to the death of the Cross! teach me to submit in all things to the dispensations of heaven.

Heart of Jesus, centre and model of all hearts! grant that mine may be pure, humble, meek, patient and worthy of thy love.

Heart of Jesus, overwhelmed with grief for the sins of mankind! grant that I may wash away mine in a flood of penitential tears.

When the clock strikes.

Grant, O Lord! that every moment of my life may be consecrated to thy service, and that I may forever love and bless thee, through the Sacred Heart of Jesus thy Son.

THE PRAYER OF ST. GERTRUDE.

Hail, O Sacred Heart of Jesus! living and vivifying source of eternal life, infinite treasury of the Divinity, burning furnace of Divine love! thou art my refuge and my sanctuary. O my amiable Saviour! consume my heart with that sacred fire with which thine is inflamed; pour down on my soul those graces which flow from thy love, and let my heart be so united with thine, that our wills may be one, and mine in all things conformable to thine. May thine be the standard and rule of all my desires and actions. Amen.

Let us pray.

LORD Jesus Christ, who hast vouchsafed to open to thy Church the unspeakable treasures of thy Divine Heart, grant, we humbly beseech thee, that we may be enriched and comforted by the heavenly graces, which constantly flow from that inexhaustible source of love and mercy. Who livest, &c.

O Almighty and Eternal God ! look on the Heart of thy beloved Son : behold the atonement and praise which it offers to thee in behalf of sinners, and being appeased by them, grant us, who implore thy mercy, pardon and peace, in the name of the same Jesus Christ thy Son our Lord.   Amen.

☞ For those whose duties may not leave time for longer exercises, we subjoin the following brief—

DEVOTIONS

TO THE

SACRED HEART OF JESUS.

"I will speak to His Heart, and I shall obtain of it all I wish." St. Bonaventure.

WE read in the authentic writings of the Ven. Marguerite Mary, these remarkable words regarding the Devotion to the Sacred Heart of Jesus: —"I say with confidence, if it were known how agreeable to Jesus is this devotion, there is not a Christian, however slight be his affection for our loving Redeemer, who would not practice it. Our Lord has shown me treasures of love and graces for those who shall consecrate themselves to give and procure for His Heart all

171

the love, honor and glory in their power. He reserves incomprehensible treasures for all, who will endeavor to establish this devotion."

GENERAL PRACTICES.

1. To enrol one's self in the Arch-Confraternity of the Sacred Heart. To receive communion the first Friday of each month.

2. To celebrate with great devotion the Feast of the Sacred Heart, and prepare for it by a solemn Novena.

3. To consecrate the month of June to the Sacred Heart. How many graces would this Divine Heart confer, if during this month the image were exposed in all churches on an altar richly adorned, as on a throne of mercy to receive our homage and hear our prayers! As Mary

is the way that leads to Jesus, so the month of Mary will conduct us to the month of the Sacred Heart.

4. Every year to place in one poor family a large image of the Sacred Heart of the Divine Consoler of all sufferings.

5. To cherish a union in all things with the Heart of Jesus, that he may supply our imperfections.

6. To spread everywhere practices, images, books adapted to increase the love of the Sacred Heart.

THE WEEK SANCTIFIED.

SUNDAY.—*Consideration.*—Devotion to the Sacred Heart has for object the Adorable Heart of Jesus, and the infinite love which it has for us. Its end is to give Him love for love, to thank Him for His benefits, and to make reparation for the outrages He

continually endures. It was revealed
to us at this time, as the most efficacious means of regenerating the
world, and re-animating in the
hearts of Christians, their wavering
faith and languid charity.

Prayers before the Image of the S. Heart

My amiable Saviour, desiring to
testify to you my gratitude, and to
repair my infidelities, I give you my
heart, I consecrate myself entirely to
to you, and propose never to sin
again. (100 days Ind., Pius VII.)
Sacred Heart of Jesus, scatter your
benedictions on the holy Church, on
her ministers, and all her children,
support the just, convert sinners,
help the dying, deliver the souls
from Purgatory, and extend the
sweet empire of your love over all
hearts. Amen. *Our Father, Hail
Mary. Glory be to the Father, &c.*

Oh! Mary, make us know the Sacred Heart of Jesus!

MONDAY.—*Consideration.*—Devotion to the Sacred Heart should not be the exclusive privilege of some pious souls. Our Lord has recommended that it be published and spread in every place. Are not all men the objects of His tenderness? Have not all men been covered with His Sacred Blood, and loaded with His benefits? Have not all wounded that adorable Heart with their sins? It is then a duty for all to bring to the Heart of Jesus a tribute of love, of gratitude, and of reparation. Oh! Jesus, exclaimed St. Liguori, make known to men the august titles you have to their love. *Prayers as above.*

Oh! Mary, make us love and imitate the Sacred Heart of Jesus.

TUESDAY.—*Consideration.*—To comprehend well the important place the

devotion to the Sacred Heart occupies
in Catholic worship, it is enough to
consider that Our Lord has Himself
asked the establishment and propagation of it: that He has determined
its principal practices, and has made
in favor of those who would consecrate themselve to it, the most consoling promises; such· as, union in
family, fervor in the service of God,
consolation in trouble, success in enterprises, and the sweetest security
at the hour of death. *Prayers as
above.*

Oh! Mary, render us zealous for
the devotion to the Sacred Heart of
Jesus.

WEDNESDAY.--*Consideration.*--Jesus
is not known enough: His love is
not sufficiently understood. It is
known. to be sure, that He is God;
that He died for us; that He is
present in the Eucharist: but He is
not known, as a child knows his

tender father ; as a friend knows his devoted friend ; He is not known, in a word, with that knowledge of the heart whence arise intimacy and confidence. Now, devotion to the Sacred Heart will make us know and love Jesus, by unveiling to us the mysteries of His mercy, the sweet influences of His love, and the maternal solicitude of His Providence. *Prayers as above.*

Oh ! Mary, obtain for us a great confidence in the Sacred Heart of Jesus.

THURSDAY. — *Consideration.* — The Heart of Jesus was formed for us : it has palpitated, prayed, suffered for our salvation, It has dictated the most moving passages of the Gospel, and instituted the Sacraments. This Heart, by its mysterious wound, has given birth to the Church, as the holy Fathers teach, and from the Holy Tabernacle it supports, directs, protects and consoles it. This Heart inspires all devotions, sanctifies all our sorrows, and gives birth to all virtues. This Heart pardons us in the Sacred Tribunal, and speaks to us in the interior inspirations of grace. This Heart, in fine, gave us Mary for our mother, and left us the Eucharist as the nourishment of our souls, and our consolation in this exile. *Prayers as above.*

Oh! Mary, make us love you as the Sacred Heart of Jesus loves you.

FRIDAY.—*Consideration.*—Our Lord expressed the desire He felt to see His infinite love honored under the figure of His wounded Heart, and surrounded with the instruments of His Passion. He has promised wherever this Image would be, it would scatter abundant benedictions. And what can the Heart of Jesus do, where He may be, but love, bless and console?—The Image of the Sacred Heart is a simple sermon, continually and pressingly inviting us to love and trust in a God, who has loved men so much. For two centuries Jesus has expressed this desire, and yet how many churches, how many Christian houses, have not the image of the Sacred Heart! How many sick, how many poor, how many afflicted souls have not before their eyes the image of this great model of resignation, of this Divine consoler! *Prayers as above.*

Oh! Mary, place us near you in the Sacred Heart of Jesus.

SATURDAY.—*Consideration.*—St. Augustine compares the Heart of Jesus to the ark of Noah, in which all that enter will be saved from shipwreck. From this open Heart escapes, says St. Cyprian, the fountain that springs up into everlasting life. The Heart of Jesus, says St. Bernardine, is a furnace of the most ardent charity, destined to inflame the universe. St,

Peter Damian calls this Heart the universal treasure of wisdom and knowledge ; St. Francis of Sales, the source of all graces, and St. Bonaventure, the treasury of all kinds of good ; St. Francis of Assisium, St. Clare, St. Aloysius, invoked it continually, as the centre of Divine love ; in fine, this amiable Heart was given to St. Mechtilda as a place of refuge during life, and as the greatest consolation at the moment of death. *Prayers as above.*

Oh ! Mary, we offer you the Sacred Heart of Jesus ; we can present you nothing more agreeable than the Heart of your Divine Son, as you have yourself declared to St. Gertrude. Receive it, then, Oh ! tender Mother, with the hearts of all your children, whose device shall ever be: All to the Heart of Jesus through the Heart of Mary !

www.ingramcontent.com/pod-product-compliance
Lightning Source LLC
Chambersburg PA
CBHW030612040726
47497CB00008B/2943